1,000,000 Books

are available to read at

www.ForgottenBooks.com

Read online
Download PDF
Purchase in print

ISBN 978-1-330-44858-8
PIBN 10063711

This book is a reproduction of an important historical work. Forgotten Books uses
state-of-the-art technology to digitally reconstruct the work, preserving the original format
whilst repairing imperfections present in the aged copy. In rare cases, an imperfection in
the original, such as a blemish or missing page, may be replicated in our edition. We do,
however, repair the vast majority of imperfections successfully; any imperfections that
remain are intentionally left to preserve the state of such historical works.

1 MONTH OF
FREE
READING

at

www.ForgottenBooks.com

By purchasing this book you are eligible for one month membership to ForgottenBooks.com, giving you unlimited access to our entire collection of over 1,000,000 titles via our web site and mobile apps.

To claim your free month visit:

www.forgottenbooks.com/free63711

English
Français
Deutsche
Italiano
Español
Português

www.forgottenbooks.com

Mythology Photography **Fiction**
Fishing Christianity **Art** Cooking
Essays Buddhism Freemasonry
Medicine **Biology** Music **Ancient
Egypt** Evolution Carpentry Physics
Dance Geology **Mathematics** Fitness
Shakespeare **Folklore** Yoga Marketing
Confidence Immortality Biographies
Poetry **Psychology** Witchcraft
Electronics Chemistry History **Law**
Accounting **Philosophy** Anthropology
Alchemy Drama Quantum Mechanics
Atheism Sexual Health **Ancient History**
Entrepreneurship Languages Sport
Paleontology Needlework Islam
Metaphysics Investment Archaeology
Parenting Statistics Criminology
Motivational

" This is a terrible piece of work."

THE LOST GOLD OF THE MONTEZUMAS

A STORY OF THE ALAMO

BY

WILLIAM O. STODDARD

AUTHOR OF "CHUMLEY'S POST," "CROWDED OUT O'CROFIELD,"
"THE TALKING LEAVES," ETC.

WITH ILLUSTRATIONS BY
CHARLES H. STEPHENS

PHILADELPHIA
J. B. LIPPINCOTT COMPANY
1898

CONTENTS.

CHAPTER VIII.

CHAPTER IX.

CHAPTER X.

CHAPTER XI.

CHAPTER XII.

CHAPTER XIII.

CHAPTER XIV.

CHAPTER XV.

CHAPTER XVI.

CHAPTER XVII.

CHAPTER XVIII.

CHAPTER XIX.

CHAPTER XX.

ILLUSTRATIONS

THE LOST GOLD OF
THE MONTEZUMAS

CHAPTER I.

THE GODS OF THE MONTEZUMAS.

IT was a gloomy place. It would have been dark but for a heap of blazing wood upon a rock at one side. That is, it looked like a rock at first sight, but upon a closer inspection it proved to be a cube of well-fitted, although roughly finished, masonry. It was about six feet square, and there were three stone steps leading up in front.

Behind this altar-like structure a vast wall of the natural rock, a dark limestone, had been sculptured into the shape of a colossal and exceedingly ugly human face,—as if the head of a stone giant were half sunken in that side of what was evidently an immense cave.

There were men in the cave, but no women were to be seen. Several of the men were standing near the altar, and one of them was putting fuel upon the fire. The only garment worn by any of them was a ragged blanket, the Mexican *serape*. In the middle of the blanket was a hole, and when the wearer's head was thrust through this he was in full dress.

There was no present need for carrying weapons, but arms of all sorts—lances, swords, bows and sheaves of arrows—were strewn in careless heaps along the base of the wall. Besides these, and remarkable for their shapes and sizes, there were a number of curiously carved and ornamented clubs. All the men visible were old and emaciated. They were wrinkled, grimy, dark, with long, black-gray hair, and coal-black, beady eyes. Withal, there was about them a listless, unoccupied, purposeless air, as if they were only half alive.

They seemed to see well enough in that lurid half light, and they wandered hither and thither, now and then exchanging a few words in some harsh and guttural dialect that seemed to have no dividing pauses between its interminable words.

Nevertheless, this was not the only tongue

with which they were familiar, for one of the men at the altar turned to those who were near him and spoke to them in Spanish.

"The gods have spoken loudly," he said. "They have been long without service. They are hungry. Tetzcatl will go. He will find if the Americans are strong enough to strike the Spaniards in Texas. He will bring them to serve the gods in the valley of the old kings. He will stir up the Comanches and the Lipans. The Apaches in the west are already busy. The gods will be quiet if he can arouse for them the enemies of Spain."

For a moment the dark figures stood as still as so many statues, and then a sepulchral voice arose among them.

"The men of the North will not come," it said. "The Texans cannot defend their own towns from the locusts of Santa Anna. The Comanches and the Lipans are scalping each other. The Apaches have been beaten by Bravo's lancers. All white men need to be hired or they will not fight. We have nothing wherewith to hire them."

A hoarse and mocking laugh burst from the lips of Tetzcatl. "Hire them? Pay them?"

he said. "No! But hunters can bait wolves. If the trap is rightly set, the wolves will never reach the bait. They will but fall into the pit they are lured to. Come! Let us look at the fire that was kindled for Guatamoczin. The Spaniards perished in the mountains when they came to hunt for the hidden treasures of the Montezumas."

Slowly, as if their withered limbs almost refused to carry them, the weird, dingy, ghastly figures followed him deeper into the cave, and each took with him a blazing pine-knot for a torch. Not one of them appeared to be aroused, as yet, to any especial interest, nor did they talk as they went. Tetzcatl, however, led the way with a vigor of movement that was in startling contrast to the listlessness of his dark companions.

There was no door to unlock, there were no bars to remove, at the end of their silent march. The distance travelled may have been a hundred paces. On either side, as they went, were stalagmites of glittering white, answering to the pointed stalactites which depended from the vaulted cave-roof above. It was a scene the like of which can be found in many another

limestone formation the world over. There
was nothing exceptional about it, only that the
specimens presented were numerous and finely
formed.

The torches flared in the strong currents of
air which ventilated the cavern, and their
smoky light was reflected brilliantly from all
the irregular, alabaster surfaces.

The sculptured head of the great idol over
the altar; the carefully maintained fire; the
presence of the aged keepers, whether they
were to be called priests of the shrine or only
worshippers, were the distinguishing features
of the place.

On went Tetzcatl until he reached a spot
where the side walls approached each other,
with a space of about thirty feet between
them. Here he paused and waited until the
others, with several who had not before made
their appearance, arrived and stood beside him.

"There!" he said, loudly, pointing with out-
stretched hand. "Guatamoczin turned to ashes
upon the coals of the Spanish furnace, because
he refused to reveal this to their greed. Know
you not that even now, if the Spaniards did
but suspect, there would shortly be an army

among the mountain passes? Aye! If the Americans believed that this were here, their thousands would be pouring southward. All Europe would come. Here is the god that they worship, but the secret of its presence has been guarded from them by the old gods of Mexico."

"What good?" asked a cracked voice near him. "It cannot be used to buy Texans. It must remain where it is until the gods come up."

"Aye! So!" shrieked Tetzcatl. "We will keep their secret chamber until they come. But the wolf does but need to smell the bait,— not to eat it. He will come, if he has only the scent. If the Texans were stirred to hunt for the gold they will never find, they would but gather offerings for the long hunger of those who dwell below."

"Hark!" responded the other speaker. "If they ask for it, it must go to them. Much has been paid them already. Hark!"

Before them, in regularly arranged rows, were a number of stacks of what seemed to be bars of metal, showing here and there dull gleams of yellow. The ingots were not large, but their aggregate weight and value would be enormous, if they were gold.

Opposite, across the passage, were other and larger stacks of ingots, but these presented no yellow surfaces. Black rather than white was the prevailing tint of what Tetzcatl had declared to be silver bullion.

Not all of the gold had been smelted and cast, for there were small heaps of nuggets, such as come from rich placer washings.

Tetzcatl had stepped forward, lifting his torch and peering into the gloom. Only a step or two beyond him, the floor of the cave was cut off, sharply, by one of the breaks or "faults" common to all rock formations, the token of some old-time upheaval or depression. The rugged level began again a few yards farther on, but there was no bridge across the yawning chasm which separated the corresponding edges. Three or four heavy planks which lay near indicated a possible means of crossing, if need should be, but no hand was laid upon them now.

The dismal-looking companions were all leaning forward in listening attitudes, intent upon a roaring, booming sound that came up from the chasm.

"They are calling," said Tetzcatl. "But we

have none to give them. Well did I say that I must go."

"It is too loud!" exclaimed the watcher, who had followed him most closely. "They have called my name!"

Tetzcatl turned quickly, but he addressed yet another of the old men by a long, many-syllabled, vibrating invocation, and added to it, in Spanish,—

"Wilt thou go down to the gods, or shall he take thy place?"

"He is gone!" was the quick but entirely unexcited rejoinder.

Tetzcatl whirled again toward the gulf, but the rock-floor at his left was vacant. The withered old devotee had not hesitated for a moment, but had plunged down headlong.

During a number of slow seconds no word was uttered, and all the while the booming roar from below diminished in volume until it nearly died away.

"The gods are satisfied," said Tetzcatl.

So seemed to think and say his associates, and they turned away to walk slowly toward the altar, as if nothing noteworthy or unusual had occurred.

It is not always easy to give satisfactory explanations of the sounds which are to be heard,
more or less intermittently, among the chasms
and recesses of great caves. The flow of subterranean waters, the rush of air-currents, the
effects of echoes, and many other agencies have
been taken into account. As for Tetzcatl and
his friends, they had but formed and expressed
an idea which was anciently universal. This
voice from the deep was but one of the oracles
which have been so reverenced by the primi-
tive heathenisms of many nations.

As for the treasure, from whatever placers it
had been gathered, its presence in such a place
required no explanation. The Aztec kings
had but exhibited commonplace prudence in
choosing for it so secure a hiding.

The cave was not at all more mysterious than
might be the underground vault of a great city
bank or a United States Sub-Treasury. It
was as safe even from burglary, if the vault-
entrance was well guarded.

More than a score of the grisly, blanketed
shapes were now gathered at the altar. Its
fire was blazing high, and shed its red, waver-
ing radiance upon their faces, while Tetzcatl

stood upon the lower of the steps and addressed them. He spoke altogether in their own tongue, and they listened without reply or comment.

When at last he ceased speaking, they all sat down upon the rock-floor, and not one of them turned his head while their exceptionally vigorous and active leader strode swiftly away in the direction opposite to the chasm and the treasure.

It was an ascent, gradual at first and then more rapid, until his walk became a climb and there were broken ridges to surmount at intervals. Before long he reached a ragged wall of rock, where the great hall of the cave abruptly ended. Farther progress would have been shut off but for a narrow cleft at the left, into which he turned. This still led upward until it became little better than a burrow. He was compelled to stoop first, and then to go, for several yards, on all-fours. Then there was an increasing sunlight, and he stood erect amid a tangled copse of vines and bushes.

Above him arose a craggy mountain-side. Below him, a thousand feet, was a wooded valley through which a narrow river ran. Along

the mountain-side, not far below where he
stood, there wound a plainly marked pathway.
With a quickness that was cat-like, he de-
scended to this path, and, as he reached it,
he looked back toward the now perfectly concealed burrow he had emerged from.

"He has gone down to the gods!" he exclaimed, aloud. "He must have Spaniards to
follow him. Tetzcatl will bring upon them
the scalpers of the plains and the riflemen of
the North. He will lure the Texans with the
gold they will never find. Ha! They will
gather none of the treasures of the Montezumas, unless the gods come up to tell them
of the sands in the secret watercourses beyond
the mountains and toward the sunset. Huitzilopochtli covered the gold gullies when the
Spaniards came."

He had a foundation of fact for his declaration. Up to that hour no search had succeeded
in accounting for the quantities of yellow metal
captured by Cortez, or for the larger deposits
declared to have been hidden from him by the
obstinate chiefs whom he had slain for refusing
to tell.

CHAPTER II

"UGH!"

Two paths came out within a few yards of each other from the tangled mazes of a vast, green sea of chaparral. For miles and miles extended the bushy growth, with here and there a group of stunted trees sticking up from its dreary wilderness. It was said that even Indians might lose themselves in such a web as that. Not because it was pathless, but because it was threaded by too many paths, without way-marks or guideboards.

At the mouth of one of these narrow and winding avenues sat a boy upon a mustang pony. At the mouth of the other path, upon a mule not larger than the pony, sat one of the strangest figures ever seen by that or any other boy. He was short of stature, broad-shouldered, but thin. His head was covered by a broad-brimmed, straw *sombrero*. Below that was a somewhat worn *serape,* now thrown

18

back a little to show that he also wore a shirt,
slashed trousers, and that in his belt were
pistols and a knife, while from it depended,
in its sheath, a *machete,* or Mexican sabre.
He carried no gun, but the saddle and other
trappings of his mule were very good. He
wore top-boots, the toes thrust under the
leather caps of his wooden stirrups, and from
his heels projected enormous, silver-mounted
spurs. His hair was as white as snow, and so
were the straggling bristles which answered him
for beard and moustaches.

He may have been grotesque, but he was
not comical, for his face was to the last degree
dark, threatening, cruel, in its expression, and
his eyes glowed like fire under their projecting
white eyebrows. He had wheeled his mule,
and he now sat staring at the boy, with a hand
upon the hilt of the *machete.* He did not
draw the weapon, for the boy was only staring
back curiously, not even lowering his long,
bright-bladed lance.

As for him, his clothing consisted of a breech-
clout and fringed deerskin leggings. His belt
sustained a quiver of arrows, a bow, and a
knife, but he seemed to have no fire-arms.

Neither did he wear any hat, and he rode his mustang with a piece of old blanket in place of a saddle.

The most remarkable thing about him, upon a closer study, excepting, perhaps, his brave and decidedly handsome face, was his color. Instead of the tawny darkness common to older Indians, he had retained the clear, deep red which is now and then to be seen among squaws and their very young children. He was a splendid specimen, therefore, of a young red man, and he had now met an old fellow of a race which had never been red. He seemed to know him, also, for he spoke to him at once.

"Ugh!" he said. "Tetzcatl. Mountain Panther. Young chief, Lipan. Son of Castro. Heap friend."

The response was in Spanish, and the boy understood it, for he replied fairly well in the same tongue.

"Good! Tetzcatl go to the Alamo," he said. "All chiefs there. White chiefs. Lipan. Comanche. Castro. Mexican. Heap fighting birds."

At the last words the face of Tetzcatl lighted up, and he touched his mule with a spur. It

"Good! Tetzcatl go to the Alamo."

was time to push forward if there was to be a cock-fight at the fort, but he asked suspiciously how the young Lipan knew him. Had he ever seen him before?

"Ugh! No!" said the boy. "Heard tell. No two Panther. Heap white head. No tribe. Ride alone. Bad medicine for Mexican. Stay in mountains. Heap kill."

He had recognized, therefore, the original of some verbal picture in the Lipan gallery of famous men.

"Sí!" exclaimed the Panther, looking more like one. "Tlascalan! People gone! Tetzcatl one left. Boy, Lipan, fight all Mexicans. Kill all the Spaniards."

From other remarks which followed, it appeared that the warriors of the plains could be expected to sympathize cordially with the remnants of the ancient clans of the south in the murderous feud which they had never remitted for a day since the landing of Cortez and his conquistadores.

Moreover, no Indian of any tribe could fail to respect an old chief like Tetzcatl, who had won renown as a fighter, even if he had taken no scalps to show for his victories.

The mustang had moved when the mule did, with a momentary offer to bite his long-eared companion, while the mule lashed out with his near hind hoof, narrowly missing the pony. Not either of the riders, however, was at all disturbed by any antics of his beast.

Tetzcatl, as they rode on, appeared to be deeply interested in the reported gathering at the Alamo. He made many inquiries concerning the men who were supposed to be there, and about the cock-fight. The boy, on the other hand, asked no questions except with his eyes, and these, from time to time, confessed how deep an impression the old Spaniard-hater had made upon him.

" Mountain Panther kill a heap," he muttered to himself. "Cut up lancer. Cut off head. Eat heart. No take scalp."

Beyond a doubt he had heard strange stories, and it was worth his while to meet and study the principal actor in some of the worst of them.

One of the old man's questions was almost too personal for Indian manners.

"Why go?" sharply responded the young Lipan. "Son of Castro. Great chief. Go see warrior. See great rifle chief. See Big

Knife! Fort. Big gun. Old Mountain Panther too much talk."

That was an end of answers, and Tetzcatl failed to obtain any further information concerning an assembly which was evidently puzzling him. They were now nearing their destination, however. They could see the fort, and both pairs of their very black eyes were glittering with expectation as they pushed forward more rapidly.

The strongest military post in all Texas was an old, fortified mission, and it had been well planned by Spanish engineers to resist probable attacks from the fierce coast-tribes which had now disappeared. An irregular quadrangle, one hundred and fifty-four yards long by fifty-four yards wide, was surrounded by walls eight feet high that were nowhere less than two and a half feet thick. On the southeasterly corner, opening within and without, was a massive church, unfinished, roofless, but with walls of masonry twenty-two and a half feet high and four feet thick. Along the south front of the main enclosure was a structure two stories high, intended for a convent, with a large walled enclosure attached. This was the citadel.

Next to the church was a strong exterior stockade, with a massive gate. There were many loop-holes and embrasures in the enclosing wall. No less than fourteen cannon were actually in position, mostly four-pounders and six-pounders.

It had been many a long year since a shot had been fired at any red enemy, for the remaining tribes, forced westward, were not fort-takers. Their incursions, rarely penetrating so deep into the nominally settled country, had reference to scalps, horses, cattle, and other plunder.

As for other Texas Indians, the Creeks, Choctaws, Chickasaws, and other "United States redskins," about eight thousand of whom were estimated to have crossed the northern border and taken up permanent abodes, none of their war-parties ever came as far south as the Guadalupe River and the Alamo.

Of Comanches, Lipans, Apaches, and the like, the old Mexican State of Texas had been estimated to contain about twenty thousand, with numerous bands to hear from in the unknown regions of southern New Mexico, Chihuahua, Durango, Sonora, and Arizona. As yet, the strength of these tribes had not been broken. They were independent nations, not recognizing Spain, Mexico, or any other power as entitled to govern them. Added to the continual perplexities of whatever authority might at any time assume to control the lost empire of the Montezumas, were sundry remnants of the very fiercest of the old Mexicans clans.

They were not understood to be numerous, but they held unpenetrated valleys and mountain ranges and forests. The boldest priests had failed to establish missions among them. It was said that no white man venturing too far had ever returned, and there were wild legends of the wonders of those undiscovered fastnesses.

During several years prior to this winter of 1835, there had been an increasing immigration of Americans from the United States. These settlers now numbered thirty thousand, or more than six times the Spanish-Mexican population, and they had brought with them five thousand negro slaves. Almost as a matter of course, they had refused to become Mexicans. They had set up for themselves, had declared their independence, and the new provisional republic of Texas, with Sam Houston for its leading spirit, was now at war with the not very old republic of Mexico, under the autocratic military presidency of General Antonio Lopez de Santa Anna.

It was toward the middle of a warm and lazy day, more like a northern October than anything that should be called winter. The sun was shining brightly upon the walls, the fort, the church, and upon the gray level of the enclosure. It was getting almost too warm for active exercise, but there was nothing going on that called for hard work from human beings.

About twenty yards from the church a long oval had been staked out, and a rope had been stretched around upon the stakes. Outside of this rope a throng had gathered which was to the last degree motley. It consisted, first, of nearly all the garrison. There were a number of other Americans, of all sorts, and half as many Mexicans, besides a few Spanish-Mexicans of pure imported blood. Not less noticeable, however, than any of the others were more than a dozen Indian warriors, in their best array, who stalked proudly hither and thither, pausing to speak only to white men of high degree. That is, they would condescend to recognize none but those whom they were willing to accept as their own equals, for the red man is a born aristocrat. At the same time they had watched as closely as had any others the exciting combats going on inside the roped amphitheatre.

These, indeed, were now completed, for their proper time had been the cool hours of the morning. It had been a grand cock-fight, almost the national pastime of the Mexicans, and decidedly popular among their red and white neighbors. Partly, at least, it had been gotten up in honor of the Comanche and Lipan dignitaries who were present, but it had drawn to the fortress the leading citizens of the nearest town, San Antonio de Bexar.

There were sentries at the open gate, of course, but there was no such severity of military discipline as would prevent any man from attending such an affair as that.

The utmost courtesy prevailed. In fact, the absolute good order was something remarkable. The lower classes might be supposed to be in awe of their superiors and of the military, but there was something more belonging to the men and the time.

Only the black men and some of the Mexican *peones* seemed to be without arms. Almost every white man wore a belt to which was secured a knife and at least one pair of pistols. Half of them carried rifles, unless, for the moment, they had leaned the long barrels against a handy wall. The bronzed and bearded faces expressed hospitality, civility, but every pair of eyes among them wore an expression of habitual watchfulness, for all these men were living in a state of daily, hourly readiness to stand for their lives. Their laws, their rights, their liberties, and their very breath depended upon their personal pluck and prowess, for here were the pioneers of the Southwest, the heroes of the American border.

Between the cockpit and the church stood a group toward which the rest now and then glanced with manifest respect. Central among them were two who were conversing, face to face.

The taller of this pair was a dark, scarred, powerful-looking savage, close behind whom stood another red man, every whit as dangerous looking but a head shorter.

The other of the talkers was a white man nearly as tall as the dark chief. He was blue-eyed, auburn-haired, handsome, and he had an almost unpleasant appearance of laughing whenever he spoke. Even while he laughed, however, his sinewy hand was playing with the hilts of the pistols in his belt as if it loved them.

"Travis," said the warrior, sternly, "Lipan fight Santa Anna,—now! What Texan do? How many rifle come?"

"Why, Castro, my old friend," replied Colonel Travis, "he is coming here. We needn't go to Mexico after him. We can clean him out of Texas when he comes in, but we won't go with you across the Rio Grande."

Castro turned and said a few words in Spanish to the shorter chief behind him, and most of the white men present understood the fierce reply that was made in the same tongue.

"Great Bear speaks for all the Comanches!" he exclaimed. "Ugh! We fight Santa Anna! Fight Travis! Fight Big Knife! No friend! Texans all cowards. Coyotes. Rabbits. They are afraid to ride into Chihuahua."

Just then, at his left, there glided near him

a new-comer to whom all the rest turned, at once, as if his presence were a great surprise.

"Tetzcatl speaks for the tribes of the mountains," he loudly declared, and his deep, guttural voice had in it a harsh and grating tone. "We send for the Comanches. We will be with them when they come. We want the Lipans to come. We ask the Texans to come. They will strike the lancers of Santa Anna and save Texas. The chiefs will take scalps, horses, cattle. Travis, Tetzcatl will show him gold. Plenty! Texans want gold."

"There isn't any gold to be found in Chihuahua," laughed Travis, "or the Mexicans would ha' scooped it in long ago. I don't bite."

"Colonel," broke in a bearded, powerful-looking man, stepping forward, "I know what he means, if you don't. He said something to me about it, once. The old tiger is full of that nonsense of the hidden treasure of the Montezumas. It's the old Cortez humbug."

"Humbug? I guess it is!" laughed the colonel. "I can't be caught by such a bait as that. The Spaniards hunted for it, and the Mexicans, too. No, I won't go, Bowie. You

won't, and Crockett won't. We should only
lose our scalps for nothing. We'll stay and
fight the Greasers on our own ground."

"Tell you what, colonel," responded his
friend, "let's have him talk it out. You just
hear what he's got to say."

"Well, Bowie," he said, "I don't object to
that, but we've all heard it, many a time. I
don't believe Cortez and his men left anything
behind them. If they found it, they just
didn't report it to the king, that's all. That's
about what men of their kind would ha' done.
Nothing but pirates, anyhow. Talk with old
Tetzcatl? Oh, yes. No harm in that."

"I'd kind o' like a ride into Mexico," remarked Bowie, thoughtfully, "if it was only
to know the country. Somehow I feel half inclined to try it on, if we can take the right
kind with us."

A ringing, sarcastic laugh answered from behind him, and with it came the derisive voice
of another speaker.

"Not for Davy Crockett," he said. "I'd
ruther be in Congress any day than south o'
the Rio Grande. Why, colonel, that part o'
Mexico isn't ours, and we don't keer to annex

it. What we want to do is to stretch out west-'ard. But we're spread, now, like a hen a-set-tin' onto a hundred eggs, and some on 'em 'll spile."

There was sharper derision in his face than in his words, aided greatly by his somewhat peaked nose and a satirical flash in his blue-gray eyes. It was curious, indeed, that so much rough fun could find a place in a countenance so deeply marked by lines of iron determination.

Very different was the still, set look upon the face of Colonel James Bowie. The celebrated hand-to-hand fighter seemed to be a man who could not laugh, or even smile, very easily.

Colonel Travis was in a position of official responsibility, and he was accustomed to dealing with the sensitive pride of Indians. He now turned and held out a hand to the evidently angry Comanche.

" Great Bear is a great chief," he said. " He is wise. He can count men. Let him look around him and count. How many rifles can his friend take away to go with the Comanches into Mexico?"

"Ugh!" said Great Bear. " Fort no good.

Heap stone corral. Texan lie around. No fight. No hurt Mexican. Sit and look at big gun. Hide behind wall. Rabbit in hole."

He spoke scornfully enough, but the argument against him was a strong one.

" Great Bear," said Crockett, " you're a good Indian. When you come for my skelp, I'll be thar. But you can't have any Texans, just now."

The Comanche turned contemptuously away to speak to one of his own braves.

" Castro," said Travis, " it's of no use to say any more now, but you and I have got to talk things over. All of us are ready to strike at Santa Anna, but we must choose our own way. When the time comes, we can wipe him out."

" Wipe him out?" growled Bowie. " Of course we can. He and his ragamuffins 'll never get in as far as the Alamo."

" Colonel," replied Travis, " take it easy. It's a good thing for us if the tribes are out as our allies."

" Hitting us, too, every chance they git," remarked Crockett. " All except, it may be, Castro. We can handle the Greasers ourselves."

Other remarks were made by those around him, expressing liberal contempt for the Mexican general and his army. They seemed to have forgotten the old military maxim that the sure road to disaster is to despise your adversary.

Tetzcatl had heard all, but he had said no more. His singular face had all the while grown darker and more tigerish. The wild beast idea was yet more strongly suggested when he walked away with Great Bear. All his movements were lithe, cat-like, very different from the dignified pacing of his companion and of other Comanche chiefs who followed them.

In the outer edge of the group of notables there had been one listener who had hardly taken his eyes from the faces of the white leaders. He had glanced from one to another of them with manifestly strong admiration. It was the Lipan boy who had ridden to the post with Tetzcatl.

At this moment, however, his face had put on an expression of the fiercest hatred. He was looking at a man who wore the gaudy uniform of the Mexican cavalry. He was evidently an officer of high rank, and he had now strolled slowly away from the completed cock-fight, as if to exchange ceremonious greetings with Colonel Travis and his friends. They stepped forward to meet him with every appearance of formal courtesy, and no introduction was needed.

"Sí, señor," he replied, to an inquiry from the fort commander. "I have seen Señor Houston. I return to Matamoras to-morrow. Our Mexican birds have won this match. We will bring more game-cocks to amuse you before long."

His meaning was plain enough, however civilly it was spoken.

"You might win another match," responded Travis, "if all the Mexican birds were as game as General Bravo."

The Mexican bowed low and his face flushed with pride at receiving such a compliment from the daring leader of the Texan rangers.

"Thanks, señor," he said, as he raised his head. "I will show you some of them. I shall hope to meet you at the head of my own lancers."

"I know what they are," laughed Travis,

"and you can handle them. But they can't ride over those walls. Likely as not Great Bear's Comanches 'll find you work enough at home. I'm afraid Santa Anna will have to conquer Texas without you."

General Bravo uttered a half-angry exclamation, but he added,—

"That's what I'm afraid of. They are our worst enemy. There is more danger in them than in the Lipans. Among them all, though, you must look out for your own scalp. You might lose it."

Travis laughed again in his not at all pleasant way, but he made no direct reply. It was said of him that he always went into a fight with that peculiar smile, and that it boded no good to the opposite party.

There seemed to be old acquaintance, if not personal friendship, between him and General Bravo, and neither of them said anything that was positively disagreeable.

Nevertheless, they talked on with a cool reserve of manner that was natural to men who expected to meet in combat shortly. The war for the independence of Texas had already been marked by ruthless blood-shedding.

General Bravo, it appeared, was even now on his return from bearing important despatches, final demands from the President of Mexico to the as yet unacknowledged commander-in-chief of the rebellious province of Texas. He was therefore to be considered personally safe, of course, until he could recross the border into his own land.

For all that, he might not have been sure of getting home if some of the men who were watching him could have had their own way, and when he mounted his horse a dozen Texan rangers, sent along by Houston himself, rode with him as an escort.

"Bravo may come back," said Bowie, looking after him, "but all the lancers in Mexico can never take the Alamo."

The iron-faced, iron-framed borderer turned away to take sudden note of a pair of very keen, black eyes which were staring, not so much at him as at something in his belt.

"You young red wolf!" he exclaimed. "What are you looking at?"

"Ugh! Heap boy Red Wolf! Good!" loudly repeated the Lipan war-chief Castro, standing a few paces behind his son.

Ugh! Ugh! Ugh! followed in quick succession, for every Indian who heard knew that the boy had then and there received from the great pale-face warrior the name by which he was thenceforth to be known, according to established Indian custom.

"Big Knife," said the boy himself, still staring at the belt, but uttering the words by which the white hero was designated by the red men of many tribes, north and south. "Red Wolf look at heap knife."

"Oh," said the colonel. "You want to see Bowie's old toothpick? Well, I guess all sorts of redskins have made me pull it out."

"Heap medicine knife," remarked Castro. "Kill a heap. Boy see."

Bowie's own eyes wore a peculiar expression as he drew out the long, glittering blade and handed it to his young admirer.

It was a terrible weapon, even to look at, and more so for its history. Originally, its metal had been only a large, broad, horse-shoer's file, sharpened at the point and on one edge. After its owner had won renown with it, a skilful smith had taken it and had refinished it with a slight curve, putting on, also, a strong buck-horn haft. It was now a long, keen-edged, brightly polished piece of steel-work, superior in all respects to the knives which had heretofore been common on the American frontier.

"Ugh!" said Red Wolf again, handling it respectfully. "Heap knife."

He passed it to his father, and it went from hand to hand among the warriors, treated by each in turn as if it were a special privilege to become acquainted with it, or as if it were a kind of enchanted weapon, capable of doing its own killing.

"Bowie, knife!" said Castro, when he at last returned it to its owner, unintentionally using the very term that was thenceforward to be given to all blades of that pattern.

"All right," said the colonel, but he turned to call out to his two friends,—

"Travis? Crockett? Come along. I want a full talk with Tetzcatl. There's more than you think in a scout across the Rio Grande. Let's go on into the fort."

"I'm willing," said Travis; and on they went toward the Alamo convent, the citadel, and they were followed by Castro and the white-headed Tlascalan.

Red Wolf was not expected to join a council of great chiefs, but he looked after them earnestly, saying to himself,—

"Ugh!   Heap war-path!   Red Wolf go!"

CHAPTER III.

NEITHER of the two stories of the solid, ancient-looking convent was very high. Both were cut up into rooms, large below and smaller above. The convent roof was nearly flat, with a parapet of stone, and it was one hundred and ninety-one feet long by eighteen wide.

In one of the upper rooms, at the southerly corner of the building, sat a sort of frontier Committee of Ways and Means, having very important affairs of state and war under discussion.

The session of the committee began with a general statement by ex-Congressman David Crockett of the condition of things both in Texas and in Mexico.

"You see how it is," he said, in conclusion. "The United States can't let us in without openin' a wide gate for a war with Mexico. Some o' the folks want it. More of 'em hold back. The trouble with 'em is that sech a scrimmage would cost a pile of money. I don't reckon that most o' the politicians keer much for the rights of it, nor for how many fellers might git knocked on the head."

That was the longest speech yet made by anybody, but the next was short.

"Ugh!" said Great Bear.

"Ugh!" said Castro, also; but he added, "Heap far away. No care much. Stay home. Boil kettle. No fight."

The next speaker was the old Tlascalan. He did not try to express any interest in either Texas or the United States, for he was a single-minded man. He declared plainly that he had come to stir up recruits for his life-long war with Mexico, regarded by him only as a continuation of Spain, and with Santa Anna as a successor of Hernando Cortez. The white rangers and the red warriors were all alike to him. Their value consisted in their known faculty for killing their enemies.

"It's all very well," remarked Travis, at the end of the old man's talk, "but we've enough to care for at home. We haven't a man to spare."

The Big Knife had been stretching his tremendously muscular frame upon a low couch, and he now sat up with a half-dreamy look upon his face.

"I'm kind o' lookin' beyond this fight," he said. "We don't want any United States fingers in our affairs. What we want is the old idea of Aaron Burr. He knew what he was about. He planned the republic of the Southwest. He wanted all the land that borders the Gulf of Mexico. We want it, too. Then we want to strike right across the continent to the Pacific Ocean. I've been to California and into the upper Mexican states on that side. We'll take 'em all. That 'll be a country worth while to fight for. Texas is only a beginning."

"Just you wait," said Crockett. "It's no use to kill a herd of buffler when you can't tote the beef. You're in too much of a hurry. The time hasn't come."

"I don't agree with you," said Travis, with energy. "What we want is Uncle Sam and a hundred thousand settlers."

"No! no!" interrupted Tetzcatl. "Gold! Show gold. Talk gold. Bring all the men from all lands beyond the salt sea."

"About that thar spelter," replied Crockett, "I'll hear ye. Tell the whole story. I've only heard part of it. Biggest yarn! Spin it!"

A great many other people had heard the

old legend, or parts of it.   It was an historical
record that Cortez had been accused before the
King of Spain of having himself secreted part
of the plunder, won during his campaigns
against the Aztecs and other tribes.   It had
brought him into a great deal of trouble, but,
after all, the fact that he had seemed to prove
his innocence did but tend to build up and
afterwards to sustain quite another explanation
of the absence of the reported gold and silver.
It had never been found, and therefore every
ounce of it was now lying hidden somewhere,
only waiting the arrival of a discoverer.

Tetzcatl was not an eloquent man, and he
spoke English imperfectly, but he was nevertheless a persuasive talker.   Somehow or other
a pebble as large as a dollar had wandered into
that room, and he put it down upon the floor,
declaring it to be the City of Mexico.   He
evidently expected them, after that, to imagine
about a square yard around it to be a kind of
map, with the Rio Grande at its northern edge
and Texas beyond.   He proceeded then as if
he had all the mountains and passes marked
out, but he had not gone far before Crockett
broke in.

"Hullo," he said. "I see. Cortez didn't find the stuff in the city, because it wasn't thar. It was up nearer whar it was placered out, hundreds of miles away."

"I never thought of that," remarked Travis. "There's sense in it."

"Bully!" said Bowie. "And all they had to do was to cart it farther."

"No carts," said Crockett. "No mules, either. Not a pony among them."

"That makes no difference," replied Bowie. "Those Indian carriers can tote the biggest loads you ever saw. One of 'em can back a man right up a mountain."

"That's it," said Crockett. "A thousand dollars' worth of gold weighs three pounds. Sixty pounds is twenty thousand. A hundred men could tote two millions. That's what I want."

"All right," laughed Travis, "but only part of it was gold. Part of it was silver. But, then, Guatamoczin could send a thousand carriers and keep 'em going till 'twas all loaded into his cave."

Tetzcatl understood them, and he not only nodded assent, but went on to describe the process of transportation very much as if he had been there. According to him, moreover, the largest deposit was within a few days' ride of what was now the Texan border. A great deal of it, he said, had not come from the south at all, but from the north, from California, New Mexico, and Arizona.

They could not dispute him, but at that day all the world was still in ignorance of the gold placers of the Pacific coast. California was as yet nothing more than a fine country for fruit, game, and cattle-ranches.

"I've heard enough," said Travis, at last. "It's as good as a novel. But I guess I won't go."

"I think I'll take a ride with Castro, anyhow," replied Bowie. "If it's only for the fun of it. Great Bear and his Comanches can have a hunt after Bravo's lancers. But it's awfully hot in here. I'm going to have a *siesta*."

That meant a sleepy swing in a hammock slung in one of the lower rooms, and the other white men were willing to follow his example.

It was pretty well understood that the proposed raid into Mexico was to be joined by

several paleface warriors. Castro wore a half-
contented face, but the great war-chief of the
Comanches stalked out of the building uttering
words of bitter disappointment and anger. He
had hoped for hundreds of riflemen, with whose
aid he could have swept on across a whole Mexican state, plundering, burning, scalping.

The Lipans and Comanches were not at
peace with each other. They never had been,
and nothing but a prospect of fighting their
common enemy, the Mexicans, could have
brought them together.

During all this time, however, one Lipan, and
a proud one, had been very busy. Red Wolf,
with a name of his own that any Indian boy
might envy him, did not need a *siesta*. He had
a whole fort to roam around in, and there were
all sorts of new things to arouse his curiosity.

The walls themselves, particularly those of
the fort and the church, were wonders. So
were the cannon, and he peered long and curiously into the gaping mouth of the solitary
eighteen-pounder that stood in the middle of
the enclosure, ready to be whirled away to its
embrasure. It was a tremendous affair, and he
remarked "heap gun" over it again and again.

He was having a red-letter day. At last, however, he was compelled to give up sight-seeing, and he marched out through the sen-tried gate with his father toward the place where their ponies had been picketed.

Great Bear and his chiefs also left the fort, but they went in an opposite direction. If there had been any thought of a temporary alliance between them and their old enemies, the Lipans, for Mexican raiding purposes, it had disappeared in the up-stairs council. Of course they parted peaceably, for even accord-ing to Indian ideas the fort and its neighbor-hood was "treaty ground," on which there could be no scalp-taking. Besides that, there were the rangers ready to act as police.

As for Tetzcatl, he and his mule were no-where to be seen.

Siestas were the order of the day inside the walls of the Alamo, but one man was not in-clined to sleep.

Out by the eighteen-pounder stood the tall form of Colonel Travis, and he was glancing slowly around him with a smile that had anxiety in it.

Near a door of one of the lower rooms of

the convent swung the hammock that contained Davy Crockett. He was lazily smoking
a Mexican cigarette, but he was not asleep.
He could see a great many things through the
open door, and he was a man who did a great
deal of thinking.

"What's the matter with Travis?" he asked.
"What's got him out thar? Reckon I'll go
and find out if there's anything up."

In half a minute more the two celebrated
borderers were leaning against the gun, side
by side, and there was a strong contrast between them.

Travis was not without a certain polish and
elegance of manner, for he was a man of education and had travelled. If, however, Crockett
was said to have killed more bears than any
other man living, Travis was believed to have
been in more hard fights than any other, unless,
it might be, Bowie. Utterly fearless as he was,
he nevertheless commanded the Alamo, and he
could feel his military burdens.

"What's the matter with me?" he replied
to Crockett's question. "Look at this fort.
If I had five hundred men I could hold it
against the whole Mexican army. That is,

unless they had heavy guns. But I've less than a hundred just now. We couldn't work the guns nor keep men at all the loop-holes."

"That's so," said Crockett. "The Greasers could swarm over in onto ye. But Sam Houston could throw in men if Santa Anna should cross into Texas. I don't reckon he'd try to haul heavy cannon across country. He'd only leave 'em in the sloughs if he did."

"That's so," said Travis. "But he's coming some day. I want to be here when he comes. I want you and Bowie and all our old crowd."

"I'll be fifin' 'round," said Crockett; "but just now I've got to go and blow my whistle in Washington. Durned long trip to make, too."

"Come back as soon as you can," replied Travis, with unusual earnestness. "I've a job on hand. Houston has ordered me to scout along the Nueces. I'll only take a squad, but it weakens the garrison. Bowie has made up his mind to take a ride with Castro. Some of the men that are not enlisted yet will go with him, most likely."

"Let him go," said Crockett. "He'll learn a heap of things. He kind o' gets me as crazy as he is about our new Southwest enterprise.

Tell you what! Just a smell o' gold 'd fetch the immigrants in like blazes. Prairie fire's nothin' to it."

" He won't smell any," laughed Travis ; but they had turned away from the gun, and were pausing half-way between the Alamo and the church. They were glancing around them as if to take a view of the military situation.

It was quiet enough now, and there was no prophet standing by to tell them of the future. What their cool judgment now told them as entirely possible was surely to come. From beside that very gun they were to see the " Greasers," as they called the soldiers of Santa Anna, come swarming over the too thinly guarded wall. There, at the left, by the four-pounder, was Travis to fall across the gun, shot through the head. Here, on the spot where he now stood, was Crockett to go down, fighting to the last and killing as he fell. In the upper corner room of the Alamo, where the conference with Tetzcatl and the chiefs had been held, was Bowie himself to perish, like a wounded lion at bay, the last man in the Alamo.

CHAPTER IV

IT was a bugle and not a drum that summoned the garrison to answer at their morning roll-call.

"Bowie," said Colonel. Travis, just after he had dismissed the men, "I don't want to ask too much. You're not under my orders, but I wish you'd take a pretty strong patrol and scout off southerly. The Lipans camped off toward San Antonio, but I'd like to feel sure that Great Bear kept his promise and rode straight away. He isn't heavy on promise-keeping."

"Not where scalps are in it," said Bowie. "He's in bad humor. I'll go."

"You bet," remarked Crockett. "Castro hasn't many braves with him. He'll be bareheaded before night if the Comanches can light onto him."

"All right," said Bowie; "but they won't strike us just now. I don't want Castro wiped out. We're old friends."

"Mount your men well," said Travis to
52

Bowie. "You may have hard riding. Don't fight either tribe if you can help it. I must be off on Houston's orders as soon as I can get away."

"I'll take a dozen," replied Bowie. "The fort 'll be safe enough just now."

No further orders were given, but he picked both his men and his horses, and he seemed to know them all.

They were good ones, the riders especially. They were all veterans, trained and tried and hardened in Indian warfare, and ready for anything that might turn up. They went into their saddles at the word of command as if they were setting out for a merry-making, and the little column passed through the gate-way two abreast, followed a minute later by their temporary commander.

The Texan rangers were armed as well as was possible at that date. The Colt's revolver had but just been invented, and the first specimens of that deadly weapon found their way to Texas a few months later. Barely two small six-shooters came in 1836, but these opened the market, and there was a full supply, large pattern, sent on in 1837.

Just now, however, each man had horse-pistols in holsters at the saddle. In each man's belt were smaller weapons, of various shapes and sizes, and not one of them failed to carry a first-rate rifle. All had sabres as well as knives, but they were not lancers. On the contrary, they were inclined to despise the favorite weapon of the plains red men and of the Mexican cavalry.

Bowie was now at the front, and he appeared to have some reason of his own for making haste.

No such indication was given, however, by an entirely different body of horsemen, five times as numerous, which was at that hour riding across the prairie, several miles to the southeastward. These, too, seemed to have a well-understood errand.

Their leader was about two hundred yards in advance of the main body, and he paused upon the crest of every " rising ground" as he went, to take swift, searching glances in all directions.

"Great Bear is a great chief!" he loudly declared. "He will teach Castro and the Lipan dogs a lesson. They have set Travis against the Comanches. Castro shall not ride

into Chihuahua.   I will hang his scalp to dry
in my own lodge.   I will strike the Mexicans.
Ugh!"

He spoke in his own tongue, and then he
seemed to be inclined to repeat himself in
Spanish, for he was an angry man that day.
It was not at all likely that he would prove
over-particular whether his next victims were
red or white, and he evidently did not consider
himself any longer within neutral territory.

Suddenly the Comanche war-chief straight-
ened in his saddle, turned his head, and sent back
to his warriors a prolonged, ear-piercing whoop.

A chorus of fierce yells answered him, and
the slow movement of the wild-looking array
changed into a swift, pell-mell gallop.

It had been a whoop of discovery. At no
great distance from the knoll upon which
Great Bear had sounded his war-cry a voice
as shrill and as fierce, although not as powerful, replied to him with the battle-yell of the
Lipans.   In another instant, the wiry mustang
which carried an Indian boy was springing
away at his best pace eastward.   Probably it
was well for his rider that the race before him
was to be run with a light weight.

Red Wolf was all alone, but if Great Bear was hunting Lipans, they, on their part, were on the lookout for Comanches. Their cunning chief had read, as clearly as had Travis, the wrathful face of Great Bear. He had camped for one night in the comparatively secure vicinity of San Antonio. Shortly after he and his braves began their homeward ride that morning, he had given to his son and to several others orders which were accompanied by swift gesticulations that rendered many words needless. What he said to Red Wolf might have been translated,—

"We are to strike the chaparral on a due south line from the fort. Ride a mile to the west of our line of march. Keep your eye out for enemies. If you see any, get back to us full speed. Great Bear has sixty braves. Maybe more. We are only twenty. He would wipe us out."

Away went Red Wolf. He was only a scout, but he was a youngster doing warrior duty, and he felt as if the fate of the whole band depended upon him. It was another big thing to add to his remarkable experiences of the day before,—a fort, guns, a grand cock-fight, and the heroes of the border,—white chiefs who were famous among all the tribes. More than all, and he said so as he rode onward, he had been spoken to by the Big Knife of the palefaces, and he had not only seen but had handled the "heap medicine knife" itself. He was now almost a brave, with a name given him by the hero, his father's friend, and he was burning all over with a fever to do something worthy of the change in his circumstances.

He was well mounted, for he was the son of a chief, and there had been a drove of all sorts to select from. The mustang under him was a bright sorrel,—a real beauty, full of fire, and now and then showing that he possessed his full share of the high temper belonging to his half-wild pedigree.

Mile after mile went by at an easy gait, and the watchful scout had seen nothing more dangerous than a rabbit or a deer. He was beginning to feel disappointed, as if his luck were leaving him. It was hard upon a fellow who was so tremendously ready for an adventure if none was to be had. He even grew less persistently busy with his eyes, and let his thoughts go back to the fort.

"Heap big gun," he was remarking to himself. "Kill a heap. Shoot away off."

At that instant his pony sprang forward with a nervous bound, for his quick ears had caught the first notes of Great Bear's thrilling warwhoop. Red Wolf went with him as if he were part of him, while he drew the rein hard and sent back his shrill reply.

"Great Bear!" he exclaimed. "Catch Red Wolf? Ugh! No! Take heap Comanche hair."

The other warriors were not yet in sight, but there was a great deal of "boy" in his boastful threat, considering the known prowess of their leader.

The sorrel pony was having his own way, and the horse carrying Great Bear must have been not only fast but strong, or he would have been left behind in short order. It was not so, however; and now, as higher rolls of the prairie were reached and climbed, the entire yelling band were now and then seen by the young Lipan.

"Poor pony!" he remarked of some of them, for their line was drawing out longer as the better animals raced to the front and the slower fell to the rear.   All were doing their best, and some were even catching up with Great Bear. It would, therefore, be really of no use for Red Wolf to stop and kill him, unless he were ready, also, to take in hand and scalp a number of other warriors.

"What Red Wolf do now?   Ugh!"

It was a question which was running through his mind hot-footed, and it was not at first easy to shape a satisfactory answer.

A white boy would have been likely to have let it answer itself.   He would have ridden as straight as he could to rejoin the band of Lipans and to tell his father that the Comanches were coming.   He would have thought only of getting them to help him in his proposed fight with Great Bear.

Red Wolf was an Indian boy.   All his life, thus far, he had been getting lessons in Indian war-methods.   He had heard the talks and tales of chiefs and noted braves in their camps and councils.   He had, therefore, been taught in a redskin academy of the best kind, and he was a credit to his professors.

"Ugh!   No!" he exclaimed, at last.   "Comanche find chaparral.   No find Lipan."

He had no need to urge his pony, but he rode southward, not eastward. Already, in the distance, he could see the endless, ragged border of the chaparral. It began with scattered trees and bushes out on the prairie. These increased in number and in closeness to each other, until they thickened into the dense, many-pathed labyrinth. The pursuers also could see, and they could understand that if the fugitive they were following was leading them toward Castro's party, they must close up to him now or never.

The whoops which burst from them as they dashed along were loud, but short, sharp, excited.

"Whoop big!" shouted Red Wolf. "Heap yell! Castro hear whoop."

He had noted that the wind was blowing in the right direction. It could carry a sound upon its wings far away to the eastward, but two very different kinds of human ears received and understood the fierce music the chasers were making.

"Forward! Gallop!" rang from the heavily-bearded lips of the commander of horsemen coming from the northward.

"Comanches! Colonel Bowie!" shouted a grizzled veteran behind him. "That's Great Bear's band, you bet!"

Another whoop swept by them on the wind as Bowie replied to him,—

"And they've struck the Lipans, I'm afraid. We must try and get into it before too much mischief's done. On, boys! We'll give him a lesson."

Silence followed, but the men looked at the locks of their rifles and felt of their belt pistols as they went forward. It was no light matter to act as police, or even as peacemakers, in that part of the world.

The other listeners were nearer and could hear more distinctly, but no sound was uttered by the warriors with Castro when their chief drew his rein and held up a hand. Every man of them knew, or thought he knew, just what it all meant, but more news was coming.

One brave who had been some distance in their rear, as a lookout in that direction, came on at full speed, followed by another whose duties had detailed him more to the westward. Both brought the same errand, for the first exclaimed, as he came within speaking range,—

"Ugh! Heap Texan," and the other, whose eyes may have been sharper, added, "Big Knife! Many rifle?"

"Comanche! Great Bear!" roared Castro, in a deep-toned, wrathful voice. "Red Wolf lose hair! Ugh! Chaparral!"

He knew that his son must in some way have been the immediate cause of that whooping, but his first duty as a leader was to save his party, letting his vengeance wait for a better opportunity. He led on, therefore, toward the only possible refuge, muttering as he went.

"Ugh!" he said. "Heap boy. Run against Comanche! Young chief! Ugh! Go to bushes. No good wait for Big Knife. Not enough Texan. Too many Comanche."

He might well be anxious concerning his promising son, but Red Wolf's hair was yet upon his head, for the wind tossed it well as his fleet mustang carried him past the outermost clump of mesquit-bushes.

"Whoop!" he yelled. "Red Wolf beat Great Bear! All Lipans get away. Ugh!"

He had not beaten his pursuer by more than two hundred yards, however, and several other Comanches were now as near as was their chief.

Could there be such a thing as an escape
from all of them? Would not the entire
swarm go in after him and surely find him, no
matter what path he might take? The situation looked awfully doubtful in spite of the
moderate advantage which he had thus far
maintained.

Closer grew the trees. Nearer to each other
were the thick "tow-heads" of bushes. On
went Red Wolf, veering to the left around
each successive cover, but seeming to push directly into the chaparral. It was a complete
cover now, and he was well hidden at the next
sharp, sudden turn that he made to the eastward.

Paths, paths, paths, fan-like, but that none
of them were straight, and fan-like was the
spreading out of the wily Comanches. Or
perhaps they were more like a lot of mounted,
lance-bearing spiders, that were going in to
catch a young Lipan fly in that web.

As for him, he had whooped his very loud-
est just before he reached the chaparral, and a
gust of wind had helped him like a brother.
Again Castro had raised a hand, but now he
shouted fiercely,—

"Hear heap boy! Red Wolf! No lose hair yet. Ugh! Whoop!"

For all he knew, nevertheless, he may have been listening to the last battle-cry of his brave son. He and his braves were at that moment riding in among the bushes, while more than half a mile away, upon the prairie, galloped Bowie and his riflemen.

"Reckon we'll git thar jest about in time to see 'em count the skelps," remarked one ranger.

"Reckon not," replied another. "Those Lipans are as safe as jack-rabbits if once they kin fetch the chaparral."

Red Wolf had reached it, but he was by no means safe. Great Bear himself had dashed in so recklessly that he and his first handful of fast racers were galloping upon the wrong paths. They discovered their error, or thought they did, in a minute or so, but a minute was of importance just then. They lost it before a kind of instinct told them to wheel eastward if they expected to find the Lipans.

That had been the direction taken by one of their best-mounted comrades on entering the chaparral, and the soft thud of his horse's hoofs had now reached the quick ears of Red Wolf.

"Ugh!" he exclaimed. "One!"

He had pulled in his panting pony, and he now unslung his bow and put an arrow on the string.

"Red Wolf young chief!" he said. "Wait for Comanche! Tell Big Knife!"

It was not altogether imprudence or bad management to let his hard-pushed mustang breathe for a few moments. It might be called cunning to let his enemies go by him if they would. But stronger than any cunning, or than any prudence concerning his horse, was his burning ambition to do something that he could boast of afterwards. What is called Indian boasting is only the white man's love of fame in another form. Each red hero is his own newspaper, and has to do his own reporting of his feats of arms.

The hoof-beats came nearer, swiftly, upon a path which crossed his own at the bushes behind which he had halted.

Twang went the bow, the arrow sped, and a screeching death-whoop followed. The Lipan boy did but prove himself altogether a son of

5

Castro when he sprang to the ground and secured his bloody war-trophy at the risk of his life. The pony and the weapons of the fallen brave were also taken. Then once more Red Wolf was on the sorrel dashing onward, while behind him rose the angry yells of the Comanches, who had heard the death-cry and knew that one of their number had " gone under."

" Ugh ! Heap boy ! Save hair !" was the hoarse-toned greeting given to his son by Castro three minutes later.

" Comanche !" said Red Wolf, holding up his gory prize. " Great Bear come. Not many braves right away. Too many pretty soon. Heap run. Ugh !"

Castro understood the situation well enough without much explanation, and his prospects did not seem to be very good. He and his braves were too few to win a pitched battle and too many for concealment.

" Ugh !" he replied to Red Wolf. " Great chief no run. Die hard. Heap fight."

The one thing in his favor was the first mistake made by Great Bear. It had kept him from being in person among the next half-dozen of the braves who had gone to the left, so very close upon the heels of Red Wolf. Even their wrath for the fate of their foremost man did but send them on the more recklessly to avenge him. They whooped savagely as they galloped past his body at the crossing of the paths. They still believed they had only one Lipan to deal with, but they were terribly undeceived, for their blind rush into the presence of Castro and his warriors was as if they had fallen into a skilfully set ambuscade. They were taken by surprise, outnumbered, almost helpless, and down they went, not one of them escaping.

Away behind them, the fast-arriving main body of the Comanches listened to the death-shouts and to the Lipan whoops of triumph, and they obeyed the astonished yell with which their leader summoned them to gather to him at the spot where he had halted.

"Too many Lipan," he said, to a brave who rode in with a kind of report. "Castro great chief. Heap snake. No let him catch Great Bear in chaparral trap. Wait. Comanche fool. Lose hair for nothing. Red Wolf heap young brave. Kill him dead."

That was indeed fame for the young Lipan warrior. Not only had he been recognized by his pursuer, but the great war-chief of the Comanches believed that the son of his old enemy was proving himself another Castro, as courageous and as cunning as his father. A mere boy, not yet sixteen, had become of such importance that he must be killed off, if possible, to prevent the future harm that he would be likely to do.

Red Wolf's ambuscade had not been of his own planning, but he had performed his accidental part of it remarkably well.

"Red Wolf, young chief! Son of Castro!" said his father, proudly. "Big Knife good medicine. Saw boy. Old friend tell name. Ugh! Good!"

To his mind, therefore, Colonel Bowie had been a kind of war-prophet, declaring the capacity of the boy he had named, giving him "good medicine," or tremendous good luck, and now his correctness as a prophet had been unexpectedly established. So said more than one of the Lipans who had been at the fort and had witnessed the performance with the wonderful medicine knife.

Now, during a number of minutes, all the chaparral was still, for even the wild creatures were hiding and the human beings talked by motions and not by spoken words. Not one of the latter, on either side, could as yet shape for himself a trustworthy idea concerning the numbers or the precise locality of his enemies. All had dismounted, however, and the hard-ridden horses had a chance to recover their wind. No less than seven of them, that had been very good Comanche ponies that morning, had now changed their tribe and had become Lipans, whether they would or not.

CHAPTER V.

AMONG THE BUSHES.

THE Texan rangers had arrived just in time to see the finish of a very fine race. They had not actually seen Red Wolf win it, but they were in no doubt as to why his pursuers made such a frantic dash into the chaparral.

"Not after the Comanches!" shouted Bowie. "Into the cover and find the Lipans! Charge!"

They went in at a point that was nearer than were Great Bear and his braves, to the spot where the Lipans worked their unintentional ambush. They heard all that whooping, and the stillness which followed it did not puzzle old Indian fighters.

"There's been a sharp brush."

"Those were scalp-whoops."

"We're in for it, boys. Shoot quick if you've got to, but hold your fire to the last minute. There are none too many of us."

Those were their orders, but there was no shooting to be done right away.

Hardly had Bowie pulled in, calling a halt,

70

in some doubt as to which path, if any, it was best for him to follow, before a sorrel mustang came out in an opening before him, somewhat as if he had been dropped like an acorn from one of the scrub oaks.

"Red Wolf!" exclaimed Bowie. "Where is Castro?"

"Big Knife, come!" replied Red Wolf, pointing rapidly. "Castro there. Great Bear there. Heap Comanches. Young chief take hair! Ugh!"

He was holding up, with intense pride, his proof that he had been a victor in a single-handed fight. To the mind of any man of Bowie's experience it was entirely correct, and he said so.

"All right," he told his young friend. "Go ahead. Be a chief some day. Now I must see your father short order. Go ahead."

It was but a few minutes after that that the Lipan chief and Big Knife were shaking hands, but their questions and answers were few.

"Glad I got here before things were any worse," said Bowie. "I can make Great Bear pretend to give it up as soon as he knows I'm here."

"Ugh!" replied Castro. "Great Bear heap lie. Say go home. Then kill horse to catch Lipan."

"Just so," said Bowie. "Of course he will. Chief, hear old friend. Do as I say."

"Ugh!" came back assentingly. "Big Knife talk. Chief hear."

"I'll keep him back while you get a good start," said Bowie. "But do you and your braves ride for the Rio Grande. Ride fast. Get back to your lodges by that way. I'll follow to-morrow with a squad."

"Ugh!" said Castro, doubtfully. "No go to lodge now. Rio long water. Where wait for Big Knife? Bravo there, along river."

"I don't exactly know just where to say," began Bowie.

"Hacienda Dolores!" sounded gruffly out of one of the bushes near them. "Across the river. Tetzcatl."

Castro almost set free a whoop in his surprise, but he checked it in time, and only exclaimed,—

"Black Panther hide deep. Good. No let Comanche see him. How Big Knife find hacienda?"

"All right," said Bowie. "I know. It's

the abandoned ranch on the other side. Pretty good buildings, too. Just as good a place as any, if I can get there with a whole skin. Reckon I can."

"Red Wolf lead horse to hacienda for Big Knife," said his father; but the voice from the bushes added, "Tetzcatl."

"That's it," said Bowie. "I'll get there. You and the youngster meet me and my men at about this place to-morrow any time I can get here. Say it 'll probably be toward noon. Now I must have a talk with Great Bear."

A chorus of friendly grunts responded to him from the Lipans who had gathered around, and they seemed to follow his instructions at once. Even Red Wolf and his pony had already disappeared.

There was a bugle among the varied outfit of the rangers, and now it was unslung by its bearer. He really knew what to do with it. As the band of white men rode cautiously forward in the direction given them, the martial music sounded again and again at short intervals. It was an announcement to the Comanches that they had more than Lipans to deal with, and it was also a plain invitation to a parley.

Just how many red foemen he might have in front of him Great Bear did not know. Neither had he any count of the white riflemen, but their presence settled his mind.

"Great Bear no fight Texan now!" was his immediate declaration to his warriors. "Heap fool Big Knife. Put him in Alamo. No see through wall. Then find Castro in bushes. No let Lipan get away."

His next business, therefore, was to ride forward, with a cunning semblance of friendly frankness, to talk with Bowie and send him back to the fort, leaving the bushes clear of rifles. Not even then did the rangers expose themselves unduly, and Great Bear knew that he was covered by more than one unerring marksman while he was shaking hands so heartily.

"Heap friend," he said. "Great Bear glad Texan come. Glad to see Big Knife. Lipan kill Comanche. Gone now."

"Great Bear lie a heap," returned Bowie, coldly. "Said he would go home to his lodge. Break word. Stay and fight Lipan."

"Ugh!" returned Great Bear, insolently. "Great Bear chief! What for Big Knife ride in bushes? Hunt Lipan dog? Take Castro hair? Shut mouth. No talk hard. Go to fort. Go sleep!"

"Heap bad talk," said Bowie, with steady firmness. "Great Bear is in a trap. Better get out. Lose all his braves. This isn't your land. Go to lodge."

The chief again spoke boastfully, and Bowie became argumentative. One of his present objects was to use up time in talk, and he was quite willing to stir Great Bear's vanity to all sorts of assertions of the right and power of himself and his tribe to fight their enemies wherever they could be found.

He was succeeding very well, and every minute was of importance to the Lipans, who were now threading their southward way through the chaparral with all the speed they could reasonably make. With the sun over-head to guide by, they could dispense with a compass. Here and there, moreover, some of them, who seemed to have been there before, found marks upon tree-trunks and branches which may have meant more to their eyes than to those of other people.

"Great Bear is a great chief," said Bowie, at last, looking at the subtle Comanche steadily.

" He has talked enough. What does he say? Will he fight now, or will he go to his lodge? —Bugle, ready!"

The bugler raised to his lips his hollow twist of brass, but a storm of " Ughs" broke out among the Comanche warriors.

Most of them had been near enough to hear the conversation. They were on dangerous ground and were becoming altogether willing to get out of it. At this moment they saw rifles cocked and half lifted. They knew that every white man before them was a dead shot, and none of them felt any desire to hear a bugle blow or a rifle crack.

The chief himself considered that he had talked long enough, and that he had been sufficiently insolent to preserve his dignity. He could therefore pretend to yield the required point.

" Good!" he replied. " Great chief go. Big Knife ride to fort. Lipan dogs run away. Save hair. Comanches take all some day. Not now. Texan heap friend. Shut mouth. Ugh!"

He offered his hand, and Bowie took it, but after that he and his rangers sat upon their horses in grim, menacing silence, while the

Comanche warriors rode out of the chaparral.
They did so glumly enough, for they had been
outwitted and they had lost some of their best
braves.

"Now, men," said Bowie, "it was touch and
go. They were too many for us if it was a
fight. We're out of it this time, but they
won't forget or forgive it."

"You bet they won't," replied a ranger;
"but I had a sure bead on Great Bear's throat
medal, and he knew it. He'd ha' jumped jest
once."

"Back to the Alamo," said Bowie. "We
must make good time."

Away they went, and in an instant the appearance of military discipline had vanished.
The leader and his hard-fighting comrades
were once more fellow-frontiersmen rather than
"soldiers." Differences of rank, indeed, were
but faintly marked upon the dress or trappings
of any of them.

There were no epaulets or sashes, but at no
moment of time could an observer have been
in doubt as to who was in command. The
roughest and freest spoken of them all showed
marked deference whenever he addressed or

even came near to the man whom Great Bear himself, with all his pride, had acknowledged to be his superior.

"Jim," said Bowie to a tall horseman who was at his side when they came out into the open prairie, "have you made up your mind to go with me into Chihuahua?"

"Go!" exclaimed Jim. "Why, colonel, I ain't enlisted. Travis can't stop me. Of course I'll go. Wouldn't miss it for a pile. It 'll be as good as a spree."

So said more than one of the other rangers when opportunity came to ask them the same question. To each the romantic legend of the hidden treasures of the Aztec kings had been mentioned confidentially. No doubt it acted as a bait, but every way as attractive, apparently, was the prospect of a raid into Mexico, a prolonged hunting and scouting expedition, and a fair chance for brushes with Bravo's lancers.

"A Comanche or Lipan is worth two of 'em," they said, "and one American's worth four. We shall outnumber any lot of Greasers we're at all likely to run against."

There was a great deal too much of arrogance and overbearing self-confidence among the

men of the Texas border, and at no distant
day they were to pay for it bitterly.

They had gone and the chaparral seemed to
be deserted, but it was not entirely without
inhabitants.

"Tetzcatl!"

"Ugh! Red Wolf!"

There they sat, once more confronting each
other, the young Lipan on his pony and the
old tiger on his mule.

"Boy heap fool," said Tetzcatl. "Comanches in chaparral. Castro gone."

"Ugh!" said Red Wolf. "See one Comanche ride away. Keep arrow."

Tetzcatl's eyes were angry. Part of his disappointment had been the renewal of the feud
between the tribes. He had hoped for their
joint help in working out his own revenges.
Nevertheless he now listened to a further
explanation, and learned that a noted Comanche warrior had no use for bow or lance just
then, because of an arrow that was yet sticking
through his right arm above the elbow. Red
Wolf could not follow him, but he had captured a dropped lance, which he was now somewhat boastfully exhibiting.

"Boy go now," said Tetzcatl. "Tell Castro, Texans gone to the fort."

"No! no!" replied Red Wolf. "Big Knife say wait. Tetzcatl wait. Hide in bushes."

No further persuasion was attempted by the old Tlascalan, although he did not conceal his preference for being without young company.

"Come," said Red Wolf. "No stay. Heap eat. Where water?"

That seemed a useless question to be asked in such a place, but there were secrets of the chaparral which were unknown to the red men of the plains. This was not their hunting-ground and never had been so. Moreover, there had been local changes and wide bush-growths during the years which had elapsed since the tribes of the Guadalupe and Nueces River country had been exterminated.

Less than half an hour of brisk riding brought Tetzcatl and his companion to the hiding-place of one of those secrets of the chaparral.

"Whoop!" burst from Red Wolf. "Old lodge. Heap water. Great medicine. Tetzcatl white head. Know heap!"

Except for its being there, unknown to

almost everybody, there was nothing ·to be seen that could be called remarkable. There were some tumbling walls of *adobe*, or sun-burned brick, of no great extent or number, near the margin of a bright-looking pond. There might be two acres of water, but no rill could be seen running into it. One that ran out, feebly, on the farther side, shortly disap-peared in the sandy soil. Red Wolf knew, for he at once rode to investigate.

"Ugh!" he exclaimed, when he reached the bit of marsh where the tiny rivulet ended. "Dead water."

A deer sprang out of a covert at the border of the marsh, but Red Wolf's bow had been all the while in his hand, ready for instant use. The bowstring twanged, the arrow sped, and in a moment more a thrust of a lance followed.

"Heap meat," said the young hunter, as he sprang to the ground and tethered his mustang.

He did not have to cut up his game unaided. Tetzcatl came to join him with his heavy *machete* already out, and he proved himself an expert butcher.

"Good!" said Red Wolf. "Where go now? Heap fire tell Comanche."

"Come," said Tetzcatl, slinging the venison across his mule, but he said no more about what he intended doing.

They rode back to the pond and around it to the southerly side. Here, scattered over several acres of open, grassy ground, were the ruins, none of them more than one-story buildings. At one place, near the middle of them, there remained almost a complete house, roofed over. Into this, leaving his mule at the door, Tetzcatl led the way. On the floor in a corner smouldered the embers of a fire, suggesting that he had been there before, on that very day. Fragments of dry wood lay near, and were at once thrown on to make a blaze, in spite of the remonstrances of Red Wolf.

"Smoke tell Comanche," he said, as the blue vapor began to curl out at an opening in the shattered roof.

"No!" replied Tetzcatl. "Small smoke. Much wind. Comanches are a great way off."

Red Wolf had to give it up, and he was very ready to enjoy broiled venison.

The best part of his unexpected good luck, however, was the water. The deer had been a sudden arrival truly, but deer were plentiful

in Texas in those days. They were to be met
with at any time, but a pond in a desert was
quite another affair.

The riding and the fighting and the after-
lurking among the bushes had consumed the
day. The sun was going down when the two
cooks in the *adobe* turned away from their dinner and carefully covered their fire-embers.
The mule and the mustang had also been doing
very well upon the grass of the clearing.
Everything was peaceful, even comfortable,
therefore, when Red Wolf remarked to Tetzcatl, "Dark come. Heap sleep. Ugh!"

"*Bueno!*" he replied. "Boy sleep. Old
man too old."

With thorough-going Indian caution, however, the son of Castro did not think of sleeping
in any house, to be found there, perhaps, by his
enemies. He took his pony with him and went
in among the bushes. Then he tied the sorrel
securely, but left him to whatever might be
coming. As for himself, no other young wolf
hunted for a more perfect cover before con-
senting to shut his eyes. Then, indeed, it was
quickly proved that the toughest kind of red
Indian boy could be completely tired out.

CHAPTER VI.

THE OLD CASH-BOX.

THE morning sun of the next day was well up in the sky before it could manage to look in over the bushes and find out what was going on around the pond and the ruins. Long before that, however, a bright young face of a dusky-red tint came to the side of a sumach-bush and peered out a little anxiously. Nothing living was to be seen excepting a mule at the end of a lariat and pin. As if satisfied by what he saw, the young redskin disappeared, but he shortly came out again, leading a pony. Another pin was driven to hold the pony's lariat, but the two animals were not picketed near each other. They belonged to different tribes and they might be at war.

Then once more Red Wolf glanced swiftly in all directions. He saw a large rabbit sitting still and looking at the mule, but he did not see any Tetzcatl.

"Heap water," he remarked, and he at once went to the margin of the pond. He took a long draught. It was pure, but he could not say that it was very cold. "Ugh!" he exclaimed, as he threw aside his weapons and took off his buckskins.

In he waded, but the pond grew deeper a few yards out, and he dashed ahead in a manner that proved him a tip-top swimmer. Such a morning bath was a rare luxury, but, as soon as he had paddled around long enough, he swam ashore and sat down to dry. Perhaps it was also for a thinking spell, and he had quite a number of things to think of. One among them came to the front pretty soon, and he put on his small allowance of clothing. Then he picked up his lance, his bow, and his arrows and walked toward the *adobe*. He found it as empty as he expected, and he at once stirred up the fire. There was plenty of venison, and he knew nothing at all about bread, coffee, and the other superfluous aecompaniments of a white man's breakfast.

What, indeed, could be better for an already celebrated Lipan warrior, intending to be a chief some day, than a whole pond of water, very nearly a whole deer, and a good fire to cook by?

He was satisfied thus far, but there was one
trait of his character which had been showing
itself ceaselessly. Red Wolf was a born in-
vestigator. It was something more than mere
curiosity. It worked well, too, with all his
training as a hunter and as a warrior, for it
led him to try and find out the meaning, if it
had any, of every thing and circumstance he
might happen to meet. His eyes were hardly
ever quiet, and they were a very keen, penetrating pair of eyes.

He broiled and ate his last cutlet, went to
the pond for a draught, and then he set himself to a close study of the ruins. He went
from one to another of them rapidly at first,
until he was able to say of them, counting upon
his fingers,—

"Heap old fort. Many lodges. No big
gun. Heap fight one day."

What he meant by that was that in several
places he had discovered skulls and bones,
which told of men who had fallen there with
none to care for their burial. Some of these
were inside of the walls of the houses. Others
were scattered in the open. All were dry,
white, decayed, ready to crumble entirely.

The first inspection had been of a hasty kind, as if for fear of interruption. When it was over, Red Wolf stood still for a moment, and stared at the openings in the chaparral. Somebody, an old man with white hair, for instance, ought to be coming out at one of them at about this time. Why did he not come?

"Great Bear in bushes," he remarked. "Heap Comanche. Big Knife come. Texan. Red Wolf want Tetzcatl."

He could not have him right away, that was plain, however much he might want him. So he turned to the ruins for another search, and this time he went more slowly, and scrutinized with greater care every square foot of each in turn.

Nothing could have been left in any of them, of course, but he was on the lookout for "sign." There seemed to be none for him to read, until at last, in one of the most completely broken quadrangles of old walls, he stood still and uttered a loud "Ugh!" of astonishment.

"Hole in wall," he said. "Heap dollar."

A considerable mass of *adobe* had been shattered in falling. Just under its former base there had been a kind of brickwork box. It had been built over so as to conceal it completely, but it had never been provided with either door or lid. In it had been placed a number of deerskin bags. One of these had split in falling, and there on the ground lay a number of silver coins. They were Spanish-Mexican dollars, halves, quarters, all more or less blackened by corrosion, exposed as they were to rain and sun, but all as good as ever.

Red Wolf had seen silver money, and any coin was to him a "dollar," but it was a matter concerning which he knew very little. It was altogether "white man's medicine," and of a very powerful kind. He knew that, at least, and his next thought was uttered aloud.

"Tetzcatl not see dollars. No find. Red Wolf talk to Big Knife. Great chief know. Heap take."

Very strong was his convictions that if Tetzcatl had at any time discovered that stuff, he would have hidden it again or carried it away. He did not regard the Tlascalan as his friend by any means, nor did he consider him as any kind of white man. Colonel Bowie was his chief just at this time, and he would know what to do with dollars. Therefore there could be no hesitation as to the right course to be pursued. Somehow or other this affair was to be reported to the Texan hero and to him only.

All that Red Wolf said or did, nevertheless, brought clearly out a well-known trait of savage character. That is, he had no clear idea of "value," and so he was not ready for "money." All of his thorough education as a brave of the Lipans had not taught him to count. He would have been as poor a hand at a bargain as if he had been a whole council of great chiefs selling half a new State to the agents of the United States.

His most exciting idea concerning his discovery was that he had found something which he believed would be of especial interest to Big Knife.

He gathered the scattered coins and put them into the hole. He lifted the uppermost bags to find out how heavy they were, but he did not open any of them. He put down the last bag that he lifted with a low-toned exclamation of "heap medicine," as if it awed him.

Only a few minutes of work were then required to cover the opening with fragments of *adobe*. After that the young treasure-finder, who did not know what he had found, turned and walked away toward the pond.

He must have been thinking of other matters while he walked, for he turned quickly and went to his mustang. Up came the lariat-pin, and once more the sorrel, after being watered was led into the greater security of the chaparral.

"No Tetzcatl come," he remarked, as he went. "Too many Comanche."

He had been a reckless, foolhardy young fellow, and he said so, in remaining so long out of cover, when he knew what enemies were hunting for him. He tethered the pony and found for himself a thicket from which he had a good view of the pond and its surroundings. No smoke was now arising from the *adobe*.

Patiently, silently, he lay and waited and an hour passed slowly by. Then he suddenly crouched lower and fitted an arrow to his bow-string.

"Ugh!" he said. "Horse foot come!"

More than one set of hoofs was falling upon the soft sand of a pathway near him, but only a faint sound was made after their gait changed from a "lope" or canter to a slow walk. At the moment when this was done four pairs of eyes were swiftly scanning the open. Low-voiced exclamations indicated that they had discovered something altogether new to them, and then they rode out from the chaparral to examine it more thoroughly.

"No Lipan," he heard them say. "No pony. Castro gone."

They had been led there by the trail of Red Wolf's mustang and the mule. They now proceeded to search for any other tell-tale foot-prints, and Red Wolf followed them with his eyes. They were not likely to discover even the fireplace, unless they should dismount. He thought of the dollars, but he believed them to be altogether safe. His most troublesome thought was his pony, for if that unwise animal should see fit to send out a neigh of inquiry to either of the Comanche ponies concealment would be no longer possible.

"Red Wolf lose hair," he said. "Strike Comanche brave! Kill a heap! Too many."

He was determined to die fighting, but his enemies were now riding out beyond the ruins, not in his direction. He was only too sure that they would come back again. It was a question of life or death that would be settled speedily, one way or the other.

Crack! It was the loud report of a rifle ringing out of the southerly border of the chaparral, and the taller of the four Comanches pitched heavily to the ground.

Loud yells of rage and astonishment were uttered by the three remaining braves, but they did not wait for a second shot. They wheeled their mustangs and galloped wildly away through the nearest opening in the shrubbery.

"Heap dead," said Red Wolf. "Ugh! Texan!"

He lay as still as before, however, during several minutes, and no white rifleman made his appearance. The slain Comanche lay on the grass where he had fallen, and his riderless pony fed quietly near him. It was only one, after all, of the numberless, unexplained tragedies of the border, and Red Wolf was too wise a young Indian to go out and hunt around for its meaning. He untethered his pony, however, and made ready for a run, if that should prove to be the next demand made upon him.

"Ugh!" he suddenly exclaimed. "Tetzcatl. No Comanche."

Out from the chaparral beyond the pond walked the somewhat mysterious Tlascalan, but Red Wolf sent toward him a kind of warning cry, as like the croak of a crow as if a very skilful crow had made it.

Tetzcatl himself might be such another crow from the response that came back. In a few minutes more he and Red Wolf were behind the same thicket, exchanging reports of their situation.

The old man seemed to care very little about the hidden rifleman or the dead warrior. Red Wolf told all other things, but he did not mention the dollars. He did, however, take note of every square inch of the white-haired tiger he was talking to, and he came very near uttering an exclamation when his keen eyes detected a stain of powder in the middle of Tetzcatl's left hand. The thought which at once arose in his mind was, " Load rifle. Powder stick on hand. Hide in the bushes. Shoot Comanche. Leave gun there. Ride around pond. Heap fool, Red Wolf. Boy! Ugh!"

It was what lawyers call circumstantial evidence, but there was no direct proof that the

Comanche had not fallen by the hand of a
Texan ranger.

"Follow Tetzcatl," said the old man.   "See
Big Knife."

Not another word did he utter, but he and
Red Wolf rode on together during about
twenty minutes side by side.

If the young Lipan expected to meet any
of the rangers or their leader at the place
named the previous day, he was mistaken.
Bowie had indeed kept his appointment, much
earlier than he had suggested, and there had
been important consequences.

Part of what had happened began to be
understood by Red Wolf when he and Tetzcatl came to so sharp a halt as they did.

Only a few yards ahead of them six riflemen sat motionlessly in their saddles with their
rifles raised as if about to fire.   The foremost
of them was apparently taking aim.

The fire flashed from pan and muzzle, and
the report was followed by a shrill screech from
behind some bushes not sixty yards away.   A
horse dashed out and off, followed by another,
whose rider also fell to the ground as a second
and third rifle cracked together.

"Load, boys! Quick!" shouted Bowie. "They haven't surrounded us, but that's what they're up to. There's another!"

The third Comanche was galloping too fast to be made a good mark of, but three bullets followed him and his pony dropped. Then it was not one of the Texans but Tetzcatl on his mule who now spurred forward. He had not gone to help anybody, for his *machete* was in his hand.

"Red Wolf, halt!" commanded Bowie. "Tell! Talk fast!"

It was not easy to obey an order that kept him from striking an enemy, but Bowie was his chief just then, and the story of the pond, the *adobe*, the four Comanches, and all other points worth telling, were rapidly told.

"Good!" said Bowie. "Tetzcatl's coming. That fellow can't give Great Bear any information. Now for the pond. What we want next is water."

The entire party wheeled away behind Tetzcatl as guide, and Red Wolf fell back among the men. He did not yet feel free to question so great a man as Big Knife, but he learned from the rangers as they rode on that their

whole party had narrowly escaped a collision
with "too many Comanches" at the spot where
they had met the Tlascalan. "We'd ha' been
wiped out sure," they said.

After that they had dodged and lurked in
the chaparral, while he went for a scouting
trip to the pond. It now seemed fairly safe
to go there, but there was no certainty as
to what had become of the main body of the
Comanches. Of course, after having broken
his agreement to go home, Great Bear felt
it to be his military duty to destroy a squad
of Texans who might otherwise report him
and bring a stronger force to punish his mis-
doings.

If the pond had hitherto been one of the
secrets of the chaparral, it was one no longer
now. Loud, however, were the exclamations
of surprise uttered by the Texans when they
rode out into the open.

"There's no telling what 'll be found if ever
the chaparral is cleared," said Bowie. "We
don't know much anyhow. Texas must be
free first, and settlers must come in."

"Colonel," said a ranger, "jest so; but no
settler's goin' to clar chaparral as long as thar's

loads o' clean prairie to feed stock on. This 'ere brush 'll stay whar it is."

"Never mind now," replied Bowie. "Water the critters and picket them where they can bite grass, beyond the walls, or as near as you can. We could hold that middle *adobe* for a while, but we're in a pretty tight kind of box."

CHAPTER VII.

THE ESCAPE OF THE RANGERS.

"IT won't do for us to hang around this place," was the substance of a number of remarks that were made by the riflemen as they cared for their horses and then followed their leader into the central building.

"Now, men," said Bowie, as they gathered around him, "the critters must have a good rest and a feed. We've run them hard. We'll get our rations right off."

All that was left of the deer began to go out of sight rapidly. Hunters like these were not apt to carry any considerable amount of provisions with them. It was not necessary in a region abounding with game. They were as independent as so many Indians, and every day's ride was expected to provide for its own evening camp-fire, with variations.

The fire blazed up; Tetzcatl and one of the men volunteered as cooks; the others were stationed here and there as outlooks, with a tendency to keep well under cover of the old walls. It may have been a willingness to be out of sight from the bushes that led the old Tlascalan to his duties at the fireside.

Red Wolf had all the while kept in the background, so to speak, but now, at last, he found an opportunity he had been waiting for.

"Big Knife great chief," he said to the colonel. "Red Wolf heap boy. Want talk."

"Come right along," replied Bowie, leading him a little aside. "Speak out. What is it? Have you found sign?"

"Heap sign," said Red Wolf. "Heap good medicine. Big Knife come, see."

"I'll do that!" exclaimed Bowie, with a sudden increase of interest. "No Indian boy was ever waked up like that without a reason for it."

Red Wolf's face was indeed "waked up," but it contained also an easily read warning when he added,—

"Tetzcatl. No good. No want him."

"I don't want him," said Bowie. "Walk slow now. Go right along."

It looked as if they were only strolling from one heap of rubbish to another. Red Wolf's leading was very direct nevertheless, and they were entirely hidden from observation when they stood in front of the covered crypt in the broken wall.

Even then not a word was uttered by either of them while the Indian boy removed some of his fragments of *adobe*. When, however, he put in his hand and drew it out full of silver coins, the sombre face of the Texan blazed fiery red.

"Heap dollar," remarked Red Wolf. "Big Knife find dollar.   No Tetzcatl."

"All right, my boy," said Bowie, but he vigorously aided in the further work of uncovering the bags.

"Ugh!" said Red Wolf.   "Heap lift."

So it was, for some of the bags were quite heavy   All were taken out, and one after another they were opened and their contents were inspected.

"Twenty of them are gold doubloons," exclaimed Bowie.   "The rest are silver.   Now Houston can buy his rifles!   There may be enough for cannon.   What he needs is the hard cash.   Why, there isn't powder enough in all Texas for one sharp campaign.   But there will be.   This is glorious!"

" Heap dollar," remarked Red Wolf.

He was not thinking of himself, therefore, but of the young republic which he and his brave comrades had created and were defending. This money, lying here, so strangely found, so entirely at his disposal, was not to be regarded as his own. Its only value to him was the service it could render in gaining the independence of Texas.

Rough, indeed, were the border men, but there are no better examples of unselfish devotion to a common cause than they were at that hour giving. Shoulder to shoulder they stood, the most unflinching band of self-enlisted volunteers that is recorded.

"There must be a good deal more than a hundred thousand dollars," said Bowie, beginning to put back the bags into the hole. "There may be twice as much, but if there is, it won't go far enough. My mind's made up. I'll go with Tetzcatl. If there's anything in that story of his, we may find the cash to fit out batteries of artillery and buy five thousand rifles."

"Ugh!" said Red Wolf. "Heap dollars buy heap guns."

"My boy," said Bowie, "you come along

with me. I'll take care of you. You shall have a rifle, pistols, knives, blankets, horses, anything you want. Now, Red Wolf, look!" He pointed at the covering they were putting on. "Heap hide! No tell! Dollars lie still!"

"Red Wolf shut mouth," was all the spoken reply, but his eyes blazed with the pride he felt over the reception of his "find" by the white hero. It was almost like being already a chief to be on intimate, confidential terms with so celebrated a warrior, with a leader whose ordinary manner was as haughty almost as that of Castro.

A few handfuls of dust, a careful wiping out of foot- and hand-marks, and then the secret of the wall was as safe as it had ever been.

Bowie, however, lingered for a moment, looking at the shattered *adobe*.

"One thing more is true," he muttered. "All that stuff was found and coined in this country. There is more where it came from, wherever the mines and placers may be. It stands to reason that the old Mexicans didn't get it all out. That makes me believe Tetzcatl! Cortez didn't, couldn't, have gotten hold of all the gold the Aztecs had above-ground when he came here. The Spaniards knew there was more. I'll go after it."

Back went the two discoverers to the cook-room and to their rations, and none who saw them come could have found upon their faces a trace of the excitement they had shown over their bags of doubloons and dollars.

Two hours later all the animals belonging to the party were feeding peacefully in the grassy open, and behind a knoll, not far from some of them, lay Colonel Bowie. His long, heavy " Mississippi rifle" was thrown forward across the knoll. Just behind him, among some withered weeds, lay the Lipan boy, as if he did not now feel willing to be far away from his white chief. He was watching him closely, and the thought in his mind almost escaped at his lips, so clear was the meaning that he read in the motions of the marksman.

" Big Knife sight deer," he thought. " Long shoot. Whoop! Comanche!"

His whoop was uttered aloud as the fire flashed from the rifle-muzzle, and the report was answered by a chorus of yells from among the dense masses of the chaparral.

" Tally one," said Bowie, coolly. " This

business is going to cost Great Bear something. I'll get a bead on him next. Six
yesterday and five to-day. I'll he still and
load up, though.   It's close quarters."

Not one of the other Texans had uttered a
word, but each was already near enough to good
cover to drop behind it, ready for long-range
rifle practice.

One feature of the situation was only too
evident, nevertheless, and there was immediate
peril of a crushing disaster.

The hot blood ran like fire through the veins
of Red Wolf. Here was a grand chance to
earn distinction. It would be worthy of the
oldest brave in his tribe. The horses! The
only hope for escape!

So like a deer he bounded from his cover
and went forward. He did not go to the
nearest horses, but beyond them, to those which
were apparently in the greatest danger of
speedy capture by the Comanches.

One of these had belonged to the brave who
was killed in the open that morning, and
another had been won in the chaparral from
his companions. They were especially valued
as prizes of war.   Up came the two lariat-pins.

Sharp jerks of the lariats called the ponies from their feeding and they followed the pulling. Louder every moment sounded the whoops from among the bushes, and arrow after arrow whizzed through the air.

" Whoop!" yelled the young adventurer. " Red Wolf heap boy! Comanches little dogs! Rabbits! Coyotes! Crows!"

It was genuine Indian glory to be able to send back such screeches of insult and derision in reply to all those arrows. Some of them narrowly missed him, although he managed to make a good shield out of the two ponies. That was the way he lost one of them, for the poor animal was shortly plunging hither and thither with an arrow through his neck.

Down he went, but Red Wolf immediately pulled up another peg, saving the noble racer of Colonel Bowie, and he therefore got in with a pair. He was met by Tetzcatl, the only man upon his feet, but he took the lariats into his own hands, remarking in a very business-like way,—

" *Bueno!* Go! Bring all! Quick!"

The remaining animals were hardly near enough to the bushes for arrows to reach them, and the red men under cover seemed to hesitate about exposing themselves.

"Humph!" growled Bowie. "They're only waiting for something or they'd dash out at him. But isn't he a buster! He'll equal his father some day. This is too bad, anyhow. All those dollars must stay where they are for a while."

Every horse was brought in without any further incident, but, for all that, the situation of the mere handful of Texans was becoming extremely unpleasant. It would, however, have been a great deal more so if they had been compelled to rely upon their own scanty knowledge of the neighborhood they were in. It was too new a country.

Colonel Bowie had not moved until the animals were safe, but he now put his fingers to his lips and blew a long, vibrating whistle. Instantly his men arose behind their covers of *adobe* or of rough ground and began to make their way to the central ruin. It was rapidly done, and Red Wolf was the last to come in, leading his own sorrel.

"We're corralled!" said one of the men.

"Not quite so bad as that," replied another; "and it'll be bad for them if they rush in."

"I reckon they're waiting for more to come," said the colonel, coolly. "It takes a good many to work a surround."

"*Bueno !*" said Tetzcatl just then. "Time to go. Beat the redskins now."

"Go ahead," responded Bowie; "we're ready."

The men mounted at the word. They had been hurriedly putting on saddles, and bridles, and now they sat like statues on horseback while he exchanged a few swift sentences with their white-headed guide.

"Forward! Take it easy !" was the next command.

Then it looked at first as if he were about to lead a charge directly into the bushes from which had come the arrows and the whooping. So complete was the appearance that several Comanches on the opposite side of the pond came out into the open. They would have been in just the right position to attack the Texans in the rear, after riding around the pond. Moreover, it seemed plain that the "surround" had been very nearly accomplished.

"That's it," said Bowie. "We've drawn 'em out. We know where they are. Now !

Gallop! Boys, it's a run, but I reckon we've euchered 'em."

He and Tetzcatl had suddenly wheeled toward the left, and not a Comanche made his appearance on the easterly side of the open as he and his men dashed into one of the widest avenues.

Fierce were the whoops and yells of the outgeneralled red men as, with one accord, they came out of their several covers to follow. Over a score were already in sight, and the yelling indicated that twice as many more were near at hand. The Texans were to run a race for their lives, but every animal that was entered for the race was in good condition, and not one of them was a second-rate runner.

"Pull in!" shouted Bowie, at the end of a quarter of an hour. "Tetzcatl says we're about safe."

"We've rid through tangles enough," replied a ranger. "How fur are we now from the south side of the chaparral?"

"Not so far as we were," replied his commander, "but we don't get out into prairie right away. You'll see what it is when you get there."

"I want to git thar, then, awful," came from another of the men. "We haven't had a scratch yet, but it's been right smart of a close shave."

So it had, and the Comanches were following upon the plain trail that was made by so many horses. Their real difficulty as pursuers was not the trail itself, by any means. Great Bear was with them now, and he had a high respect for the men he was dealing with. A number of minutes had been lost to him at the outset by the make-believe charge. After that, as his gathering band rode on, the prudent chief compelled his eager braves to draw rein several times at places where the thick "tangles" suggested the possibility of an ambush and a deadly volley of rifle-bullets. It was really a pokerish business to follow dead shots, men of desperate courage, too, among those dense coverts. He was a wise chief, no doubt, but every time his foremost warriors paused to reconnoitre the white men gained additional time.

Red Wolf all the while kept somewhat diffidently in the rear. He was, after all, only a boy among great warriors. Before long, however, he found himself riding at an easy gait side by side with Colonel Bowie, and the Big Knife was holding out something.

"Young brave!" said he. "Want good knife? Present."

It was one which had been found in the belt of the first Comanche warrior killed in the open, and there had been no claimant for it. It was a very good knife, longer than most others, although not shaped altogether like a bowie. Its sheath was silver-mounted and its edge was keen. It was worth a dozen of common butcher-knives such as the one Red Wolf now carried, and his eyes glistened with pleasure. It would be a war-trophy to show to his father, and all his tribe would envy him so fine a weapon. Its greatest value, however, even to them, would be the fact that it was a battle-token given by the great single-hand knife-fighter of the white men.

"Ugh!" exclaimed Red Wolf. "Heap knife. Great chief give! Whoop!"

He secured it in his belt, and then his old butcher-knife was contemptuously transferred to a place among the fringes of his leggings.

The Texans were not using up their horses,

but no halt was made. They went steadily forward for several miles of winding way, and then the chaparral began to change its character. Instead of mere bushes there was heavy timber with much undergrowth, and the land grew rugged and rocky instead of sandy.

Tetzcatl was continually several yards in the advance. He now turned and beckoned, spurred his mule, and seemed almost to vanish.

" Forward, men !" shouted Bowie. " I know what he means! I've been bothered by that very ravine more than once. It runs almost to the Nueces River. Hurrah! Great Bear won't run his braves into such a death-trap as that is. Come on !"

A number of fine old oak-trees stood like sentries grouped around the mouth of a kind of chasm, with rocks on either side. There was a descent at once, and the ravine grew deeper as the rangers rode farther into it. Tetzcatl was ahead of them, but the mule plodded on without waiting for anybody, while his rider turned and put a finger on his lips.

Not a shout was uttered, therefore, to tell how glad they all were to get into that ravine, and Bowie almost instantly exclaimed, in a low voice, to the long-legged Texan who was riding near him,—

"Jim Cheyne! Look! That's what he means. That head, up there at the cliff-edge, among the rosin weeds. Can you fetch him? Long range, but I'll try. One of us may hit."

"Ready! Together!" answered Jim, and in a few seconds more the two rifles cracked almost like one.

Tetzcatl had watched the marksmen, and now he nodded approvingly and rode on, but no one climbed to the upper level to inquire whether one bullet or two had cut short the scouting of the imprudent brave, whose eagle feather had betrayed his weedy lurking-place.

It was, nevertheless, another proof that Great Bear was a great chief and that he knew that country, for he had sent his scouts in the right direction before trying to close in upon the Texans at the pond. He had even guessed correctly at one of their possible lines of escape. He could not have calculated beforehand that a feather and a head with a bullet in it should give so complete a confirmation.

"He won't go back to tell," said Bowie, "but we shall be followed all the way."

CHAPTER VIII

"CROCKETT, there isn't any use talking. We've an awful tough job cut out."

The old bear-hunter had stuck his coonskin cap upon the muzzle of his rifle, and he stared up at it for a moment.

"Reckon we have," he said; "but we kin skirmish around the corners of it somehow. I've been in tight places before now, but I allers crawled out or fought out."

"We'll have to fight out this time," said the large, determined-looking man he was talking with. "But what on earth are we to do for money?"

"We're played out," replied Crockett, thoughtfully. "We've borrowed all we could. We've taxed till we can't put on any more. Uncle Sam won't let us have any. Houston, we're in a hole."

"The worst of it is right here," continued Houston. "If the legislature lays a tax, all the cash is appropriated before it's collected.

What I want is some money to spend without
giving any account of it.   We want a powder-
and-lead fund.   I've spent all I had."

"You kin skin my pile," said Crockett.
"Wish thar was more of it.   We're torn down
poor.   We might almost be whipped by Santa
Anna for want of money to keep the men in
the field.   Think of losing the Alamo!"

"I couldn't help it just now if we did,"
groaned Houston.   "It's safe yet."

"'Tis till somebody comes to take it," was
the ominous response of Crockett, as he lowered
his rifle and put on his coonskin.   "Just as I
told ye.   Travis is off on his scout with half
the garrison.   Bowie went on that expedition
of his, and I hope he may get back.   Thar
isn't enough powder in the fort to fire all the
guns more'n twice 'round.   No provisions to
speak of.   No nothin'.   If Greasers enough
came, they could a' most walk right in."

"They're not ready to come yet," said Houston; "but they're coming, Davy!   There 'll
be blood when they get in as far as the
Alamo!"

"You bet thar will!" shouted Crockett,
springing to his feet.   "I mean to be thar

when they come. We kin hold it ag'in' all
Mexico if we've men and powder."

The two Texan patriots were not in any
house. They had been sitting side by side
upon a log not far from a rail-fence corner
where their horses were hitched. From what
they said it appeared that they had met there
by appointment. It was as good a parlor as
such men needed to discuss affairs of state in.
Houston had now risen, and they were walking
toward their horses.

"Crockett," he said, " it's time for me to git
up and git. You go on to Washington. See
what you can do. Inquire about rifles and
cannon and ammunition."

" Well," replied Crockett, " money's the best
kind of am'nition, but we needn't forget one
thing. Santa Anna feels a kind of bowel grip
right thar. He can't fetch as many rancheros
as he'd like to cross the Rio Grande with. He'd
ruther 'tend a cock-fight any day than meet
us in a shootin' match, onless he was ten to
one."

" I wouldn't mind four to one," said Houston, " but I would mind being cut up for lack
of powder to shoot with."

"You bet!" said Crockett, bitterly. "Think of bein' jest murdered by Greasers!"

They had reached their horses, and in a moment more they were steadily galloping northward.

A very undefined domain was the vast region to which the Spanish conquerors had given the name of Texas. They had never thoroughly explored it, nor had they determined its boundaries. Its northerly line was that of the then French province of Louisiana, and that was as uncertain as the weather. It might be said to begin at the Sabine Pass on the sea-shore. From that it was supposed to wander inland. The United States surveyors had made their own maps after Jefferson purchased Louisiana from Napoleon, but they had no direct French or Spanish help.

Westward, Texas was believed to have a limit somewhere among the as yet unvisited mountains and plains. No line had been fixed on that side. Southward, the old Spanish maps, and afterwards the Mexican copies of them, were at variance as to whether the Nueces River or the Rio Grande marked the Texas border. This was of less consequence so long as Texas should belong to Mexico, but, a few years later, those conflicting maps played an important part in bringing about the war with the United States. All of that record belongs to history, and so does the older claim that Texas never, at any time, belonged to Spain, but was, in part at least, French territory, and was sold to the United States, accordingly, along with Louisiana.

It is history now, but that history had not been made up when, late that day, Colonel Bowie and his men rode out of the long ravine and found themselves upon an open prairie. It was dotted here and there with groves of oak. Much more interesting at first to the mounted marksmen was the fact that it was also dotted by several small droves of wild cattle.

"Buffalo!" exclaimed Bowie. "I didn't think of meeting any here. We must have one. Then we'll go into camp as soon as we can find water."

"Ugh!" came instantly from the Lipan boy. "Red Wolf find heap water."

"Bully!" said the colonel. "This used to be a Lipan hunting-ground. Go ahead. Find us a good spring."

Red Wolf had his orders and off he went, while Jim Cheyne looked after him and re-marked emphatically,—

"That young chap's going to be a buster. But now, boys, don't let's load up too much with meat. One good critter's all we want."

"All right," replied one of his comrades; "but, Jim, if we keep our hair on overnight thar won't be any time wasted on huntin' to-morrow."

"We shall strike straight for the Nueces, and then for the Rio Grande," said Bowie. "Great Bear hasn't let up on us, and we must look out for him all the time. He's just death on a trail."

"You kin swar to that," added Cheyne. "He's as ready to ride into Mexico, too, as we are. How's that, Tetzcatl?"

"*Bueno!*" snapped the dark-faced panther. "Comanches find Bravo's lancers beyond the river. Kill them all."

He gave no reason for the resentful feeling he had shown against Great Bear, but loud chuckles among the men expressed their ap-proval of his idea that if the Comanches should meet the lancers the story of the Kilkenny cats would be repeated.

A general hunt was forbidden on account of the horses, and only two men went out as buffalo butchers.

On leaving his party, Red Wolf rode in a kind of long circuit instead of aiming at the nearest grove. He galloped a full mile before he gave any reason why he had not gone in a straight line. He may have been a little uncertain about his landmarks, but he made no considerable error in his calculations.

"Ugh!" he exclaimed, as he pulled in upon the crest of a prairie roll and looked forward earnestly. "Heap hole. Big stone. Big Knife get water."

He was near the brink of a deep and remarkable hollow. It was almost regularly funnel-shaped, and on the opposite side of it sat a large boulder of granite. Such "sink-holes" can be found only in limestone formations. They are supposed to lead to caverns and subterranean watercourses. The presence of a mass of granite was, therefore, one of the many puzzles for geologists. Perhaps it had floated there upon a cake of ice. Then the ice had melted; the water had run off down the sink-hole; and the boulder was left to supply the red hunters of the plains with a perpetual guide-board.

"Big stone here," he said.   "Water there."

The direction in which he rode away gave his words an explanation.   He went as straight as an arrow for more than another mile, hardly glancing aside, either at groves of trees or herds of fat bisons.

Meantime, the white men he was providing refreshment for rode slowly onward.   They heard a brace of rifle reports, and took the success of their hunters for granted.   They remarked to each other, however, that good luck was with them, for "bufler" were getting scarcer year after year so far as that to the eastward.

"One of these days," said Bowie, "they'll all be gone.   This 'll be corn land then, and every farmer 'll raise his own beef."

"He'll kill it for himself, too," laughed Cheyne.   "I don't want to be here then.   I'd ruther have my beef runnin' round the prairie for free shootin'."

Bowie's eyes were all the while busy in a search for "sign."   He had found none near his present line of march, but if he could have looked back upon his entire trail he would have seen several things to interest him.

The first point was in the timber at the upper end of the long ravine. A dozen braves of the Comanches were grouped, on foot, around the opening through which Tetzcatl had so suddenly disappeared. They were watching, bow in hand, as if it had been the den of some wild animal, or rather as if, possibly, some returning Texan might at any moment show himself as a target.

Not far down the ravine, but on the upper level on one side of it, three more braves sat in silence by the body of their tribesman who had been slain by the bullet of Cheyne or Bowie. Every now and then they peered over into the gorge below and listened as if for the sounds of horse-hoofs upon the gravelly bottom. Watchers had been set, therefore, to intercept any returning ranger. That was only by way of precaution, in case of an escape from the other part of the relentless pursuit.

Miles and miles away, along the route of the winding cleft and on its westerly side, rode twice as many Comanches as had been with Great Bear when first he had been seen by Red Wolf, on the plain beyond the chaparral, two days before. His reinforcements had arrived and he was ready for extensive mischief.

At point after point, wherever the ravine was approachable and descent into it fairly easy, a warrior on foot, sometimes even on horseback, would go down and search any soft earth at the side of the little rill at the bottom. Then he would swiftly return, report that he had found the trail; that Bowie's men were farther down, all of them; and the band would ride steadily on.

Of course, this did not mean rapid riding, but it did mean a deadly and persistent pursuit. It meant a bloody revenge for slain warriors.

One brave was now sent back after the squad of watchers, but Great Bear's force was a very strong one without them. Yet other braves were riding fast and far in the advance.

Sooner or later it was sure that such a following, by trailers so skilful and so determined, would bring them near enough for a sweeping blow. What could half a dozen rangers and one Lipan boy do against the overwhelming rush of a hundred and fifty warriors?

Red Wolf did not actually come back to his white friends. He only rode near enough to whoop to them and to wave his lance, as if inviting them to follow.

"That's high!" exclaimed Jim Cheyne. "We might ha' hunted for water all night if it hadn't been for him."

"It takes an Indian sometimes," replied the colonel. "But this crowd won't make a long camp on this prairie."

"You bet!" came from several voices at once, and away they rode after the young Lipan.

It was a very pretty place for a camp, when they came to look at it. Nearly an acre of ground was occupied by tall, old sycamores and spreading oaks, and outside of these were bushes. In the middle of all was a fine spring, from which a tiny brooklet rippled out into the plain. Close around the spring the ground had been trodden hard by the hoofs of many generations of buffalo and deer, but there was plenty of grass without picketing their horses outside of the grove.

"Boys," said Bowie, "if Great Bear should find us, he'll have braves enough to corral us in such a place as this. They could just ride around and around, out of shot, and pen us in till we starved."

"That's so," put in a short, bandy-legged ranger whom the others had called "Joe," without troubling themselves to add any other name; "but I reckon we won't wait to be penned in. What I'm a-thinkin' of jest now is bufler hump."

He had the entire sympathy of his hungry comrades, and they did not have to wait long. The fire was hardly up in good shape before the two hunters rode in, bringing the best pieces of a fine "bufler."

"Now we're all right for rations," said Jim Cheyne; "but I'd like to know what's went with that young Lipan wolf."

Every man glanced quickly around him, but the son of Castro was nowhere to be seen. He had been as ready for his supper as any white man, but stronger than anything else was his feeling that he was on his first war-path. He was a brave of the Lipans, with a new name and a new knife. He had already won some glory and he was burning for more. As for even buffalo "hump," a Lipan warrior who

could not go without his dinner had never yet
been heard of.

He had mounted silently, therefore, and had
galloped away, straight back, along the line
by which he had first come to the grove and
spring. He and his pony had been watered,
and the latter had nibbled a little grass, but
that was all.

" Comanche come to hole," he said to himself, as he rode along. " Red Wolf see."

The plan in his head seemed to include nothing more than scouting duty, but this was of a
peculiar and dangerous kind.

The shadows were deepening in the groves
and on the prairie when Red Wolf reached the
sink-hole, but he was able to examine it carefully. The sides of the funnel-shaped hollow
were not too steep in some places, and he led
his mustang half-way down. He picketed him
there, upon a slope where he could stand, a little uncomfortably, and pick grass, which was
greener than any on the outside prairie. As
soon as this was cared for, Red Wolf went up
again and stationed himself by the boulder.
There was quite enough granite for one watcher
to hide behind.

"Ugh!" he said. "Texan too much fire. Comanche find camp. Where Big Knife?"

It required eyes like his to detect, at that distance, a few faint sparks which had floated up above the trees and an exceedingly dull glow of light that was just then showing.

"Texan heap fool!" he exclaimed. "Great Bear come. Ugh!"

He hardly did his white chief justice, however, for Colonel Bowie was even then ordering the fire to be smothered as soon as the needful cooking could be done. There would be no more sparks nor any glow to betray the camp.

"Colonel," said Joe in reply, "it's all right, but we'd better jest lop down and snooze. Mebbe it's all the chance we'll git for a nap."

"Snooze away," said the colonel; but Jim Cheyne was looking around him, and he suddenly exclaimed,—

"I say! What's become of that thar old tiger? He didn't go off with the Lipan cub."

"No," said Joe. "That he didn't. He was 'round yer chawin' bufler meat not five minutes ago. I heerd him say something 'bout his mule——"

"Mule's gone," came from a ranger who had

stepped away to look for him. " Tell ye what, boys, that thar old rascal's gone back on us."

" I reckon not," replied Bowie, after a moment of consideration. " He hasn't gone to Great Bear, but we shan't see him again till we get to the Hacienda Dolores. Red Wolf's gone scouting."

" That's his best hold," said Joe. " Glad he went; but they'll get him if he doesn't watch out sharp."

That was precisely what he was doing, as he crouched behind the boulder, almost as motionless and silent as the stone itself.

CHAPTER IX.

THE SKIRMISH IN THE NIGHT.

THE great gate stockade at the southeastern corner of the Alamo, near the church, was closed. There seemed to be no patrol outside of the wall and all was quiet within, but a solitary sentry paced to and fro at the gate, with his rifle over his shoulder. He was considering the situation as he walked, for he remarked, as if to the shadows around him,—

"This yer fort is pretty much taking ker of itself, but the Greasers don't know it. Thar ain't any of 'em nigh enough to come for it, anyhow. Ef they did, what thar is of us could give up this 'ere outside cattle-pen and retreat into the fort. We'd hev to give up the church, but we could garrison the Convent till help got yer. That's all we could do."

At that moment his rifle came down, for he heard a sound of hoofs that ceased in front of the gate. Out went the muzzle of his piece at a shot-hole, and he looked along its barrel as he demanded of the rider,—

128

"Who goes thar?"

"Sam Houston!" came loudly back. "Open quick! I'm followed!"

"Boys!" yelled the sentry. "It's old Sam himself! Come on! I'll git the gate open!"

"I met Crockett!" shouted Houston. "He's all right. But I've about ridden this horse to death. Down he goes! They're coming! Lancers!"

Several pairs of hands were busy with the massive bars of the portal, and two of the men had stationed themselves by the six-pounder gun that stood there, facing it, like an iron watchman.

Outside, the general stood by his fallen horse, calm and steady as a tree, with a heavy pistol in each hand.

"I've barely distanced them," he said. "Ready, boys! Give 'em something!"

Excepting for the sound of their horses' hoofs Houston's pursuers were making no noise, but they were now dangerously near him.

Open swung the gate, and the men who opened it could see the glitter of lance-heads in the moonlight.

"Step in, gineral!"

"Jump now!   Git out o' the way!"

"Quick, Sam!   I want to let 'em have it. Git inside!"

Altogether unceremonious were the rough men of the border in their hurried greetings to the man whom they really loved and trusted above other men.   He did not seem to hurry, however.   It was with a great deal of natural dignity that he strode through the gate-way. He was willing to escape the thrusts of those lances, but he felt no throb of fear.

He was safely away from the range of the six-pounder, and that was all, when the report of the sentry's rifle at the shot-hole was followed instantly by the roar of the cannon.

"It was pretty much all the grape we had," said one of the cannoneers, "but I reckon we kin load her once ag'in.   Hope we gethered some on 'em."

It had been short range, just the thing for grape-shot.   The lancers had not dreamed of such a greeting as that in the night, at the very moment of their supposed success.   They had felt all but sure of striking a blow which would have been to Texas like the defeat of an

army. They had followed their intended vic-
tim fast and far. In tracing his movements
from place to place, and in this final dash for
his life, they had exhibited more than a little
daring and enterprise.

They were barely a minute too late at the
end of their long race, but they were just in
time to be struck by that deadly storm of
grape-shot. Down went horses and men.
Down went flashing lance-points and fluttering
pennons, while loud cries of pain, and execrations, and shouts of astonishment told how
terrible had been the effect of "about the last
grist of it that we had in the fort."

"Load up, boys!" said Houston. "Close
the gate. That's all there is of that crowd."

"Thar they go, what's left of 'em," replied
the sentry.

The fort had not been left without an officer,
however, and another voice shouted,—

"Steady! Men! Lanterns! A detail of
six. I'll go out and see what we did with that
grape."

The lanterns were already coming, and Houston himself marched out with the detail. He
stooped to look into the face of a Mexican who

had fallen several paces in advance of the others.

"Colonel José Canales!" he exclaimed. "Well, boys, Santa Anna has lost one of the bravest men in his whole army. I'm glad he hasn't many more like him."

"Eight killed and three wounded, counting him in," responded a ranger. "It's the uniform of the Tampico regiment. Canales took his best men for this hunt. Mr. Houston, you've had a narrow escape this time. You mustn't ever do it ag'in. You ort to be locked up. You'd no business to run such a risk!"

"Why, boys," said the general, "I was uneasy about the fort. Crockett told me more than I knew before, and I came right on to inspect."

"Inspect thunder!" exclaimed the officer in command, a slight-looking fellow in a buckskin shirt and tow trousers for uniform. "Thar isn't much to inspect. What we want is more men and more rifles, and more powder and lead."

"Tell you what, Houston," added the gunner who had fired off the grape, "don't you know? If the Greasers came into Texas, this is the first p'int they'd make for. They'll want it bad."

" What's more just now, gineral," shouted a half-angry ranger, " 'twasn't your place to lose yer skelp a-comin'. The rest o' the boys feel jest as I do. You mustn't try on sech a fool caper ag'in. Texas can't afford to throw ye away 'bout now. Ef you was wiped out things 'ud go to pieces."

The protests of the brave riflemen were exceedingly free, but they were utterly sincere. They were freemen, talking to a man who perfectly understood them. He therefore apologized, explained, promised faithfully to do better next time, and they let him up.

Far away, beyond the belt of chaparral and the long ravine, another Texan patriot, as devoted as Houston, sat by his covered camp-fire in the grove, and it seemed as if he were echoing the words of the garrison of the Alamo.

" Arms and ammunition," he said. " There won't be any lack of men if we can feed 'em. But a Mexican with a *machete* or a lance might put under a rifleman out o' powder."

He was silent for a moment, and then he added,—

"I mustn't get myself killed on this trip. If I do, Houston 'll never know about that pile in the *adobe* hole. I'll be more careful than I ever was before."

He was not noted for special care concerning his personal safety, but he now arose and went around the camp, from man to man and from horse to horse. He seemed to be all alert, watchful. There was to be no surprise of that camp for any fault of his.

It was now getting well on into the night. Only a little earlier there had been a slight movement of the shadowy form that was crouching at the side of the boulder at the sink-hole.

"Ugh!" muttered Red Wolf, but he said no more, as he peered eagerly over the rock.

Only such ears as his could have caught a few low sounds that floated toward him on the night-wind. They were cautiously-spoken words in the Comanche tongue, and the speakers were within a hundred feet of him.

"Sink-hole," he heard them say. "No Texans there. Big Knife took them to the water. Go bring Great Bear. We find Big Knife."

There he lost several words, but it was plain

enough.   These were only an advance party.
They had sent a brave back to guide their main
body, and were themselves to ride on to make
sure of the Texans being at the camp-ground so
well known to Indian hunters.   One of their
number was to remain at the sink-hole.

"Trap Big Knife?" thought Red Wolf.
"No.   Heap eye.   Texan sleep.   Great chief
wait for Comanches."

He evidently had great confidence in his hero,
and he hardly breathed while several horsemen
went by, leaving a solitary brave to mount
guard at the outer side of the boulder.

He was very near.   It was almost certain
that before long he would discover whatever
might be living near him if it moved.   It
would be useless, therefore, for Red Wolf to
try to escape on foot that he might warn the
camp.   It would be even greater folly to go
down into the sink-hole after his mustang.
It was hardly safe, at first, to risk the slight
motion required in fitting an arrow to the
string.   He must wait, he thought.   But if
he did, what about the Texans if Big Knife
should lie down and go to sleep?   Even that
small party of Comanche warriors might dash

in and take a scalp or stampede the horses. They were very dangerous fellows on a war-path or prowling around an enemy's camp.

"Ugh!" exclaimed the Comanche, wheeling his horse and lowering his lance.

Red Wolf's mustang had not been at all comfortable down there in the dark. He had picked grass and he had stepped up and down at the end of his tether. He had heard hoofs go by. Now he was aware of the presence of another horse near him, and he sent up short neighs of inquiry. He uttered the mustang words for,—

"Hullo, pony, who are you?"

The Comanche at once responded,—

"Where are you? Hey?"

"Horse in hole!" exclaimed the warrior. "Where Texan? Where Lipan?"

He listened a moment, and again the animals spoke to each other.

"Ugh!" said the Comanche. "Texan go away and leave pony. Go take him. Heap brave!"

It was a piece of reckless daring, indeed, to go down alone into that blind hollow. There might be something much more dangerous than a pony lurking there. Again assuring himself, however, that he was a great brave and afraid of nothing, he sprang to the ground. He tethered his own pony, laid aside his bow and lance and club and drew his knife. He adjusted his shield upon his left arm, and then he was ready.

His worst peril was not in the hole. While he was making his rapid preparations Red Wolf made his own. His arrow was in its place now, and he was almost lying flat at the corner of the boulder.

There was not light enough for long-range archery, but now the Comanche brave stepped stealthily forward, knife in hand, his shield up, and his short, hard breathing testifying his intense excitement. He slipped along past the rock.

"Twang" went the Lipan boy's bowstring, and he sprang to his feet, drawing his own knife as he did so,—the splendid present of Bowie, the white hero.

Loud, fierce, agonized, was the yell of the stricken warrior, but even in his agony he whirled around to face his unexpected assailant. He had strength yet, for he sprang at Red Wolf like a wounded wildcat.

Away darted the son of Castro, but his
enemy, a man of size and muscle, was close
behind him.   But that he was already mortally
hurt he would have made short work of the
young bowman.

Back and forth among the shadows bounded
and dodged the ill-matched combatants.   Red
Wolf had no shield, and his knife glanced
more than once from the smooth, hard bison-
hide of his opponent's round buckler.

"Ugh!" screeched the Comanche at the end
of a terrific minute, and he sank into the
grass.

He had done his best, all the while failing,
but now the end had come, and Red Wolf
shortly walked back after the horses.   His
own mustang was led out of the hollow, the
Comanche pony, a fine one, was taken possession of, with his late owner's weapons and ornaments and the much-prized trophy of victory.

"More Comanche come pretty soon," he
exclaimed.   "Red Wolf take hair.   Tell Big
Knife.   Tell Castro.   Who-op!"

Never before had he sounded so loudly, so
triumphantly, the war-cry of his tribe, but the
whoops which answered him did not come from

" Ugh !" screeched the Comanche at the end of a terrific minute, and he sank into the grass.

the direction of the camp. They arose from the northward and told of many whoopers.

As for the scouting-party, if any of them had turned back to assist their comrade at the sink-hole, they as yet were silent. So was Red Wolf now, as he galloped away into the darkness.

The camp was too far away for even a death-whoop to reach it, but Colonel Bowie's tour of guard duty had led him out at last to a tuft of sumach-bushes, beyond the easterly border of the grove.

Here he stood, looking out somewhat listlessly, but before long he uttered a low, sharp exclamation, and brought his rifle to his shoulder.

"They've come!" he said. "I must rouse the boys. It's life or death this time. How they tracked us here I don't know."

As he glanced along the rifle-barrel he could see dim forms on horseback glide between him and the starlit horizon. They were at no great distance, and he turned to send into the camp a piercing whistle. It reached the ear of every ranger, asleep or awake. Even the horses seemed to understand that it was a note of alarm, and they began to step around as if they were in a hurry to get their saddles on. They need not have been in any anxiety, for when the men sprang to their feet, rifles in hand, their first care was for their four-footed comrades.

An immediate reply to Bowie's whistle came also from away out on the prairie.

"That's the warning whoop of the Lipans," he said to his men. "Red Wolf is out there somewhere. Hope they won't get him. He shouldn't ha' whooped."

But Red Wolf had not been unwise, after all. The Comanche scouts were few in number and they had no desire to be caught between two fires, Lipans, if there were any, on one side, and the riflemen on the other. They therefore dashed ahead, and then nearer, louder than before, the Lipan yell sounded again.

"That's a startler!" exclaimed Bowie. "It isn't the boy! It's a grown-up screech."

Another of the full-sized startlers came, and a third, a fourth.

In, however, without any more whooping, galloped Red Wolf himself, with his prizes and his pride and his exceedingly important news.

Closely behind him followed yet another horseman, coming at speed, and, in a moment more, Bowie stood face to face with Castro, as the Lipan chief, springing to the ground, strode forward and held out a hand.

"Big Knife here?" he said. "Good. Lipans at Hacienda Dolores pretty soon. Castro ride back on trail. Find friend. Heap talk by and by."

"All right, chief," said Bowie. "But the Comanches are here. Let Red Wolf tell what he found. Quick!"

Very rapid indeed was the young warrior's account of his performances, and Castro seemed to be growing taller in his glorification over such a feat done by his younger self.

All who heard could fully appreciate, and Red Wolf had quite as much praise as was good for him.

"Chief!" said Bowie. "Men! It's mount and ride now. Heap the fire. Pack the bufler meat. Fill the canteens. Get a good ready."

He and Castro had more questions to ask and answer while the swift preparations went on, and Red Wolf was thoroughly cross-examined.

There were no additional tokens of enemies near the camp, but if the scouting-party had discovered that the Texans were on guard, another party of Comanches, halted at the sink-hole, knew that they had lost a comrade and that he had fallen by the hand of an Indian. The Texans did not use arrows nor take scalps. It was a matter for thoughtful consideration, to be reported to Great Bear.

"Ready now," came at last in a low voice from Bowie. "Mount! Lead ahead, chief. We can get a good start of 'em before day-light."

It was well to have Castro for a guide, but it was mainly due to Red Wolf that they dared to stir out of camp and cover at all. But for the information he brought of the exact situa-tion, prudence might have bidden them to re-main and fight behind the trees, in the belief that overwhelming numbers were around them.

As it was, no Comanche knew of the depart-ure from the camp. Even when the first rein-forcements arrived, all that the red cavalry deemed it well to do, without the personal presence and orders of Great Bear, was to ride slowly around the grove and make sure that nobody in it should have a chance to get away. The fire was blazing high, and they thought of what marksmen among the trees and bushes were ready to shoot by the light of it. There was nothing to gain by over-haste, and they waited.

All the while, across the southward prairie, Bowie and his men rode on, and now they knew, from Castro, that General Bravo and his lancers had been seen along the line of the Rio Grande.

" We can keep out of his way," said the colonel, " but, next thing to outracing Great Bear, I want to get a sight of Tetzcatl. I reckon he'll kind o' come up out o' the ground just when we don't expect him."

" Ugh !" said Castro. " Heap snake. Heap lie. No want him."

CHAPTER X

THOSE were dark days for Texas. Too many of the white settlers were new arrivals, who as yet were in a strange country and had not made up their minds as to what leadership they would trust. There was, indeed, a strong central body of veterans who rallied around Sam Houston and General Austin. They were the right men for a battle-field, but they had very little ready money.

Thus far, in fact, very nearly the best protection for the young republic had been given by the disordered condition of public affairs in Mexico. At last, however, the ablest man south of the Rio Grande, General Antonio Lopez de Santa Anna, had so completely subdued the several factions opposed to his supremacy that he deemed it safe for him to lead an army for the recovery of the rebellious province at the north.

144

There were those who said that in so doing he ran a serious risk of losing whatever he might leave behind him, especially in case of a defeat, but the pride of the Mexican people had been aroused and there was a clamorous demand for action.

There had all the while been war, in a scattering aimless way, and there had been threatening embassies, like that recently accomplished by Bravo.

How to invade Texas, nevertheless, was a question to puzzle an invader. There were not many points or places in the vast area the Americans were seizing that were of military value. An invading army would but waste its time in marching around or in camping on the prairies. It must find a Texan army and defeat it or go home useless.

One of the few points of importance, in most men's opinion, was the Alamo fort, but it was really little more than a convenient rallying-place. Apart from that, a scientific general would have said that it was nothing but a piece of ground which had been walled in. It was worth blockading, perhaps, but it was not worth a hard fight.

The Texans themselves did not think so, nor did the Mexicans. To the Texans it had a certain value as a stronghold, and they took much pride in it on that account. The Mexican generals were possessed with an idea that it was Texas itself and that it would be absolutely necessary to take it.

General Houston, making a careful inspection of the fort and its surroundings the morning after his arrival, was deeply impressed both with its importance and its weakness.

"Boys," he said, "if this place had rations enough and powder enough in it you and Travis could hold it all the year 'round."

"Jesso, gineral," responded a ranger; "but if they fetched big guns, they could knock them walls to flinders."

The walls looked very strong, and his comrades disagreed with him, but Houston shook his head and walked to the eighteen-pounder in the middle of what some of them called the "plaza."

"This would do," he said to himself, "but Santa Anna won't drag in any guns like this as far as the Alamo. He can't take this fort with nothing but ranchero lancers and field-guns. I must get some money somehow and put things in order, but where I'm to get it I don't know."

He went in then to eat his breakfast, and not long afterwards was riding away, with a sufficient escort to protect him from being murdered before he could get out of the town of San Antonio de Bexar.

In the dawn of that very morning a cloud of wild horsemen had gathered upon the open prairie between the sink-hole and the grove where the little party of Colonel Bowie was believed to be still encamped. That from it came no sign of life was of no importance whatever to warriors who knew how perfectly the rangers were skilled in all the cunning of bush and forest fighting.

A mist had covered the rolls and the hollows, but the smoke of the camp-fire could be seen. Once a log fell, sending up a shower of sparks, and Great Bear himself remarked that Big Knife's men were putting on more wood. He now had with him the greater part of his force, but every pony was tired, and some of them had given out entirely.

There was no special reason for haste, excepting the water of the spring for men and beasts. Perhaps the better way would be to obtain a parley and induce the Texans to come out of their ambush before slaughtering them. A little cunning might accomplish that, and so the Comanches waited.

Of course, the grove was surrounded to prevent any sudden dash for escape, but shortly after the rising sun began his work upon the mist the encircling force moved slowly nearer. The main body moved together until they were about a hundred yards from the outer shrubbery. Then they halted, and a single brave, a chief of rank, dismounted and went forward on foot, holding out his right hand with the palm up, in token of a wish for truce and conference.

The eyes of his band were upon the messenger and he walked steadily, although all the while believing himself to be covered by the unerring aim of Texan sharp-shooters. His nerves were very good. No sooner, however, did he reach the trees than Great Bear and his column moved forward again.

On strode the solitary herald of peace, or of treachery, but no rifle cracked, no mustang neighed, no Texan came out of a bush. It was the strangest affair, to the mind of a man who was absolutely sure that his enemies were there.

On he marched until he stood by the fire at the spring, and glanced fiercely around him. It was too much! His hand went to his mouth, and he uttered a whoop which brought every Comanche within hearing pell-mell toward the grove.

Such a rush would have been their best chance for crushing Bowie's men in any case, but the charging warriors found no Texans to crush. Wild were the whoops of wrath and disappointment, but Great Bear himself was equal to the occasion. His face expressed strong admiration of such a feat of generalship, and he said, loudly,—

"Ugh! Big Knife great chief! Get away heap! Comanche tired now. Find Texan by and by."

There was no help for it. The only thing to do was to rest and to eat, for immediate pursuit was out of the question.

Miles and miles away, an hour or so later, in another camping place as good as the one they had left, the white riflemen also were taking it easy. They had plenty of buffalo cutlets to broil; they had distanced their pursuers, and they were contented.

"Boys," remarked Colonel Bowie, "we've gained a whole day's ride on 'em if we work it right."

"All right, colonel," responded Joe; "but when that young Lipan rid in last night I begun to wish I was back in the Alamo. My skelp felt loose."

"He's a buster," remarked Jim Cheyne; "but I'm right down glad his dad is here. Best guide we could git."

As for Red Wolf himself, he was sitting apart from the rest. After all, he was only a boy and all these others were distinguished warriors.

CHAPTER XI.

DAYS that go by with nothing in them but steady riding, buffalo-killing, and undisturbed camps at the end of each day may be very pleasant but they are not exciting. As Colonel Bowie remarked to his men, however,—

"A squad like ours, mounted as we are, can get ahead faster than a big band like Great Bear's. They'll send scouting-parties ahead, but we can keep out of their way. We're making first-rate time."

So they were, and they were also carefully keeping their horses in good condition for any required run. They carried no baggage, and they had now, they thought, a long "start" ahead of their Comanche pursuers.

The most silent rider among them, not excepting Castro himself, was Red Wolf, and it was not altogether because he was a boy. The fact was that he had been seeing and hearing a great deal, and that he was full to bursting with the spirit of adventure which all the while spoke out in the talk of the Texans.

They told wild stories of old war-paths; of fights of every kind, and of visits to cities and towns of the white men. They talked, too, about gold and silver and what could be done with money, so that the young Lipan grew more and more interested in an idea he never had before,—the idea of riches. It did not yet take complete shape in his mind, excepting in one form, given by Big Knife, the hero. It was what he said about the great gun in the plaza of the Alamo, and the money it would cost to kill Mexicans with that and the other cannon. The "heap guns" themselves had cost a great deal of money. In that shape, or even in the shape of rifles or horses, Red Wolf could now understand it fairly well. He thought of the bags in the hole in the *adobe* wall, but these, he believed, belonged to Big Knife and the Texans. They could not be the property of a Lipan boy, and he never thought of such a thing for a moment. Very vaguely, moreover, he had gathered that this present war-party expected to find gold and silver and to bring it back with them, after killing enemies and winning glory in fights.

It was all new and it was all wonderful, but there was no use in talking about it, so he kept still and was inclined to ride ahead, or else to linger some distance behind his party.

As yet there had been no sign of any pursuers near them, but toward the close of one long, bright day Red Wolf had fallen so far behind that he was almost out of sight of his pale-face friends.

The swift mustang under him was in fine condition. So very well did he feel that he was restive, and a deer that sprang out of a covert of hazel-bushes as he was going by made him jump and throw up his heels. Not that he was at all afraid of a deer, but that it was curious, perhaps, to find himself carrying a hunter who would not so much as send an arrow after such capital game.

"Ugh!" exclaimed Red Wolf, and it came out sharply, from utter surprise.

In his sudden prancing his pony had wheeled around, and there, coming over a rise of ground not two hundred yards away, rode three Comanches. The instant they were discovered they uttered fierce whoops and dashed forward.

"Wh-oo-p!" yelled the young Lipan, lashing his too spirited pony to a run. "Comanche dog! Red Wolf!"

There was no more to be said just then, however. The warm wind from the south seemed to whistle past him. Far to the right and far to the left yet other war-whoops were sounding. Not the whole band of Great Bear, he thought, but a sufficient number of their best mounted braves to make trouble for Bowie and his men.

There is no such thing as mistaking a war-whoop for any other sound, and now Red Wolf exclaimed "Ugh!" again in still greater astonishment. He knew that there was no bugle among the Texans with Big Knife, but he had heard the sound of one at the fort and afterwards. "Heap whistle" would have been a good translation of his Lipan word for bugle music, and he uttered it loudly. It came from the left, and it was faint at first, but in a few moments it was repeated more sonorously, and he wheeled his mustang in that direction.

At that very moment Castro himself, riding

at the head of the squad, lifted his left hand
as if pointing and exclaimed,—

"Ugh!   Big Knife hear!   Mexicans!"

"It's a cavalry bugle, colonel!" shouted Jim
Cheyne.   "I can ketch it.   Thar it comes
ag'in——"

"Wheel to the right!   Gallop!" replied
Bowie.   "It's Bravo's lancers.   They are this
side of the Rio!   Now, boys, the chief was
just saying we were only a half-hour's ride
from the hacienda.   His Lipans are there."

Were they?   It is not always that a man
can give the whereabouts of other men from
whom he has been several days absent.   A ride
of half an hour is also to be measured by the
speed of a horse, rather than by feet and inches.
Very near them, therefore, if the distance were
that of a swift horse on a run, a mule and his
rider had halted on the northerly bank of a
broad and very muddy river.

Directly across the river, on a low bluff of
seemingly bare, sandy ground, there was a long
range of low-built houses, part of them surrounded by a wall.   They were altogether like
a vast number of other Mexican-Spanish *haciendas*, or head-quarters of important country

estates. If this, however, were the Hacienda Dolores, and if Castro's Lipans were there, they had raised over the largest of the *adobe* structures the eagle flag of Mexico. They had stationed uniformed sentinels here and there, and they had picketed horses, with saddles and military trappings, in long rows near at hand.

"Tetzcatl counts more than four hundred," said the man on the mule. "The Lipans are safe, but the Mexicans must not catch Bowie."

He spoke in Spanish and his voice was quiet enough, but his face was all one quiver of rage and hate as he stared across the river. What if his entire plan was to be broken up and his red and white allies destroyed by this unexpected activity of his Mexican enemies? It was, moreover, a dangerous place of waiting for a solitary old man, to whom no quarter would be given if he were found there by Mexican soldiers.

"Too long! Too long!" he exclaimed. "They ought to be here. It is time!"

At that moment the mule under him stretched his neck and head to send forth a loud and seemingly uncalled-for bray. He had an abundance of ears, but what could he have heard? His white-headed master at first heard nothing at all, but then he drove his spurs into the sides of his trumpeting beast in a way that cut off braying.

"Bowie!" he shouted. "Running. He is trapped by Bravo's men!"

There, indeed, racing as if for life, were the six Texans and Castro, but where was their young Lipan scout, and what was he doing?

Castro was asking that question, and so was the colonel, only the moment before, but now they pulled in their horses to look across the river, in blank dismay, at the flag over the hacienda.

"They've got us this time, colonel!" roared a broad-chested ranger. "Our call has come. Let's die game!"

"You bet we will," said Joe, "but we ain't dead yit. Something's a-goin' on away back yonder. I heard an Injin yell sure's you live."

If he and his friends had not been running away so fast they might have heard a number of Indians yell.

Red Wolf had ridden toward the bugle, not away from it. Hardly three minutes of so

swift a run had been required to bring him
out in full view of a strong party of mounted
men in the brilliant uniform of the Mexican
regular lancers. It was just as they obeyed
the musical order to go forward at a charging
gait. They were splendid horsemen and they
moved together in perfect array, but it was not
to make a dash upon one Indian boy. They
had some reasons for expecting an encounter
with the band of Lipans which had quartered,
during several days, in and around the deserted
hacienda. Here these were now, they thought,
apparently ready to be pounced upon and
overwhelmed, but this nearest brave upon the
mustang showed no sign of hostility. On the
contrary, he pulled in, almost halted, and waved
his hand to them before pointing back, as if he
would say,—

"Your enemies and mine are there. Be
ready for them."

Swift orders rang along the charging column,
but the solitary Indian wheeled out of their
way, still making friendly signs, while over
the swells of the prairie came the wild riders
of whom he was evidently telling.

To him no more attention could be given

just then, for there were more Comanches arriving than Bowie had believed at all likely. They had travelled faster and in better condition than he had calculated, and fully a third of Great Bear's warriors were within reaching distance.

It was a tremendous surprise all around. The fast-gathering braves had expected to close in upon a mere handful of tired-out Texans. The lancers had counted upon a brush with a small war-party of Lipans. Here the two forces were, however, face to face, altogether too near to escape a collision, unless one side or both should lose courage and run away.

Red Wolf had lashed his mustang to its best speed in wheeling from between the combatants, and he barely succeeded, for the Comanches were careering in various directions. It was not their custom to charge in close column.

"Ugh!" said the boy warrior. "Heap fool Comanche. See Great Bear."

The great war-chief was indeed among his men, as cool as ever in spite of the surprise. He had his best braves with him, and they greatly outnumbered the Mexicans. The latter, indeed, rather than the red men, had stumbled into a bad place. They were brave enough, but the Comanches have been called by army officers "the best light cavalry in the world." Not one of them turned to follow Red Wolf any farther, and he did not wait to be followed. He looked behind him only to catch a fleeting view of a terribly confused skirmish. Both sides carried lances. At close quarters, the bows and arrows of the red men were even better weapons than were such fire-arms as were carried by the cavalry. It certainly took less time to load a bow-string than it did to put a charge into a horse-pistol or a carbine.

The Mexicans were fighting well, Red Wolf could take note of that. What he did not see was the fact that they were going down very fast and that more Comanches were arriving. The one idea in his mind was to overtake his friends.

The river! The great, muddy Rio Grande! Here it was, with not a sign of Colonel Bowie's party upon its desolate bank.

Red Wolf halted in something like dismay, but it was no time for hesitation. His friends

could not have gone down southward. Their
errand would lead them up the river. He must
hunt for them in that direction. Whether he
should ever reach them or not was a difficult
question, as his first glance across the river
told him. It was not so much the flag on the
hacienda. He was not afraid of a flag. But
the river was shallow and fordable at this point,
and a party of lancers had already made its
way well out from the farther shore. They, as
well as he, could hear the rattling reports and
the fierce whooping from the battle that was
going on, and they were making as much haste
as the muddy bottom permitted. They uttered
loud shouts when they caught sight of the one
"brave" on the bank, and they fired shot after
shot at him, but he was out of range of the
short, smooth-bore carbines they were firing.
He answered them with a yell of derision and
rode on.

"Ugh!" he said. "Heap Mexican! All
lose hair. Great Bear come."

Even a Lipan boy could feel more exultation
than anything else over the idea that one enemy of his tribe was doing much harm to another. As an Indian, moreover, he could be

proud of the prowess of a chief like Great
Bear, almost as great a man, in his estimation,
as Big Knife or as Castro.

It was a hot skirmish, but it was a short one.
Half the lancers were down, but their charge
had carried them through the unsteady swarm
of their enemies. All that were left were keeping well together and were galloping toward
the river, followed by flights of arrows. They
would have been more closely followed by wild
horsemen but for the fact that the Comanche
ponies were at the end of a long, tiresome
"push," while the animals of the cavalry were
fresh. There was no such thing as catching
up with them, and they reached the bank just
as their comrades from the opposite shore were
wading out.

There were loud shouts of explanation.
There were signals to and from the hacienda,
but all that could be done was to recross the
river. After all, Red Wolf had not won any
glory, but his enemies had once more suffered
severely in trying to get hold of him.

CHAPTER XII.

THE HORSE-THIEVES AND THE STAMPEDE.

"BOYS," said Colonel Bowie, sitting upon his panting horse and looking back down the river, "they saw us. I don't think we could make another run. Dismount!"

They were barely a mile and a half above the point where they had struck the Rio Grande, but it was time to give their horses a rest and to consider the situation. They had halted on the brow of a bluff, and they were looking in all directions. Not a man of them could guess from what quarter their next disaster might come.

"Big Knife wait," replied the Lipan chief. "Castro go back for Red Wolf."

"Guess not!" exclaimed Jim Cheyne. "Colonel, if thar isn't that thar old cuss Tetzcatl on his mule."

Here he came, plodding along as calmly as ever, but there was very little news that he could tell them. He could not even explain the presence of General Bravo's regiment of lancers.

"The general said, at the Alamo, that he was going after the Apaches," remarked the colonel, "but here he is."

"Whoop!" rang out from the lower ground easterly. "Who-o-o-oop!"

"Red Wolf!" exclaimed Castro. "Boy no lose hair! Ugh! Heap young brave!"

On he came, and there was no one following him. How could he have escaped? He tried to tell how when he reached them, but before he had finished his story of the Comanches and the lancers Tetzcatl turned his mule toward the river.

"*Bueno!*" he said. "We can cross here. The lancers are busy. So are the Comanches. The Lipans are on the other side and we can find them. Come!"

"All right!" shouted Bowie. "Forward! Boys, Great Bear is our best hold just now. He got in just in the nick of time."

The chief himself had not said so, nor had the beaten lancers. Both sides of that fight had been severely surprised.

It seemed to the Comanches that their long

chase had reached a stopping-place, and what
to do next they could not say, except to rest
their horses. As for the lancers, what was left
of the fighting party was now safe at the
hacienda.

The Texans had no choice but to follow their
white-headed guide. Not one of them heard
him say, as his mule waded into the river,—

"*Bueno!* The Comanches got them. It is a
great satisfaction. I will take the Texans into
the mountains and give them to Huitzilopochtli.
They shall go down to him when he calls for
them. The gods are hungry."

There had, indeed, been vast changes in the
manner and amount of worship paid them since
the landing of Cortez. There had been a time
of fanatical devotion before that, when from
twenty thousand to fifty thousand human victims had been sacrificed annually to the terrible
divinities of the Mexicans. The scattered remnants of the old, dark tribes, who still clung to
their heathenish faith, might be as ready as
their fathers had been to offer sacrifices, but the
offerings were not so easily to be provided.

"The days have been too many," grumbled
Tetzcatl, "in which not one Spaniard stood

before the altar. We have had to give them mission men, women, children. They shall have six white men from the North."

Those Mexican Indians who, from time to time, had nominally accepted the religion brought to them by the missionaries of the Church of Rome were not to be classed as Spaniards exactly, but they would answer as less valuable substitutes. Perhaps they were really as available for sacrificial purposes as had been the yearly prisoners of war, entirely un-converted heathen, who had been slaughtered at the *teocallis*, or idol temples, before any Spaniards were to be had.

Altogether ignorant of the religious fate intended for them, the Texans gained the southerly bank of the river, but their guide did not pause there. He spurred his mule, waved his hand to them, and pushed onward. He was upon ground that he knew, and their weary day's journey ended in a dense forest, where they could believe themselves safe, for the time, from their enemies.

"Night come," said Castro to his son. "Red Wolf go see Mexicans. No take horse."

"Ugh!" replied the young warrior. "Find lancers. See hacienda. Where great chief go?"

"Castro find Comanches," replied his father. "Big Knife keep camp. Tetzcatl hunt Lipans. Texan sleep."

It was a time for vigorous scouting, but the condition of the horses required that the scouts should use their own legs. No one went out at once, however. After a hearty supper they all lay down for a while. All but Tetzcatl. Nobody could say just at what moment the old Tlascalan disappeared, leaving his mule behind him.

"Boys," remarked Joe, "we're all here and we ain't corked up, but thar isn't a blamed thing we can do. It's been a pretty tough kind of spree far as we've gone."

"Wall, ye-es," drawled Jim Cheyne, "and thar's no tellin' what 'll turn up next."

"Jesso," came from another ranger, "and we needn't crow loud. Thar wouldn't ha' been a head o' ha'r left among us if it hadn't been for that cub o' Castro's; he's a buster."

"So's his dad," remarked Jim; "but whar are they now?"

He was looking, as he spoke, at the spot where he had seen them spread their blankets. Those were there, but neither a young Lipan nor an old one.

"They ain't in this camp," said Joe, after a wider search. "Gone visitin'?"

They had not gone together. A very little later the chief was wading into the river at a place somewhat below where Tetzcatl had led them across, and he was alone.

His son was at the same time slipping along among the bushes and trees toward the Hacienda Dolores. He was making rapid headway, and his bright, black eyes were dancing with excitement. Fatigue was a thing he seemed to know little about. Probably it had rested him to sit down long enough to eat his supper.

The old hacienda had a number of lights burning in it that night, and there were camp-fires kindled here and there outside of the wall for the lancers. There were a few tents, but the greater part of the force was compelled to bivouac upon its blankets. The Comanches were known not to have crossed the Rio Grande, and there was no fear of a night attack, so that only the ordinary sentries and patrols had been posted. The most important of these were in charge of the "corral," where the cavalry horses were picketed, and with them a large drove of half-trained mustangs which had been gathered to fill the places of such animals as were from time to time used up by reckless riders. The rancheros are horsemen, but they are almost horse-killers in their merciless spurring.

"Heap pony!" said Red Wolf to himself, when at last he was able to crawl along the ground, within watching distance of the corral. " Mexican bad eye. Lose pony. Great Bear send brave. Ugh!"

An indistinct shadow was moving along not many yards from him. Another lay very still a little farther off, but this latter shadow was the body of the sentry who had gone to sleep on his post. There was no one there now but Red Wolf to note the passage of several more shadows, not in uniform. He crept a little farther and lay still in a hollow. He hardly breathed, for it was equally dangerous to retreat or to go forward.

"Lie down heap," he thought. "See what

come. Ugh! Comanche bring horse. Pin pony. Go back for more."

That was precisely what had been done by the daring and expert red horse-thieves. They were unsurpassed in that line of business, and they had made their selections with care. Only the best of the animals tethered near that point by the lancers had been selected for removal.

Nevertheless, the red men were few. They could not spare a sentry. They did but secure their first string of prizes by lariats and pins before they went in for another lot.

"Big Knife want horse," remarked the young Lipan to himself. "Red Wolf take. Comanche lose pony."

It was short creeping, and then the pins were out and the string of stolen quadrupeds was once more in motion. Their feet hardly made a sound upon the sand as they went. They were led on to the shelter of some bushes, and there Red Wolf left them that he might once more snake his way back to his perilous post of observation. It seemed like going to almost certain death, but he worked his stealthy way along until he could see a tall warrior, leading several ponies, come to a sudden halt at the place where the first captures had been left.

"Ugh!" exclaimed the warrior. "Heap pony gone. More braves come take 'em. Good. Take more pony."

He believed, therefore, that his own tribesmen had been there, but at that moment a shrill "Who-o-o-op" sounded from the darkness near him. Almost unconsciously, or from the force of habit, he replied to it with his own war-cry. Following that came a dozen more from within the corral. One after another, in quick succession, every Mexican sentinel fired off his musket in sudden alarm. A bugler caught up his bugle and began to blow it loudly. It was a hubbub of mingled sounds, but the warriors in the corral sprang each upon the back of the nearest pony and plied his whip savagely upon the frightened animals around him. Horses neighed, mules brayed, red men whooped, cavalrymen shouted, and the net result was a wild stampede of every brute that was loose or that could break his tether. Of course, they all ran after the first to get away, and these had struck out into the open country.

It was no time for Red Wolf to care what became of the drove, the hacienda, or the Comanches. He had retreated after sounding his mischievous whoop, and he was now on the back of one of the stolen horses, with the others following patiently in a string behind him. They at least had escaped being stampeded, and at the same time a large number of their four-footed comrades were on their way to the river under the care of the successful warriors of Great Bear.

There was no danger that General Bravo's crack regiment would be in pursuit of anybody very early the next morning.

The night was indeed nearly gone when Jim Cheyne, standing sentry for the Texans, was hailed from among the bushes,—

"Red Wolf! Want Big Knife. Bring pony."

"Colonel," shouted Jim, "here's that buster boy again. He's been stealing ponies from the Greasers. He'll do."

"He will!" exclaimed Bowie, springing to his feet and coming forward.

In a few minutes more he said it again, and so did they all with emphasis, but the colonel added, gloomily,—

"It's almost sun-up, boys. What I want is to hear from Tetzcatl and Castro and the Lipans."

"Glad we've a lot of fresh mounts, anyhow," said Joe. "What we need most is to be able to git away."

"We will go to the river-bank first," said Bowie. "Castro is to meet us there. Even Tetzcatl believed the Lipans had gone across the river."

"If they did it's all day with them," replied Cheyne, but Red Wolf did not at all understand him. He was just then, under Colonel Bowie's instructions, selecting for his own use the very best of the fine animals he had so daringly captured and brought to camp.

The camp-fires were soon blazing, but little time could be given to breakfast. Their present position was too perilous. Parties of lancers would surely be out, and there were too many of them. Besides, there were the Comanches, and no man knew when or where they might make their appearance.

It was bright morning when the little cavalcade, with its fine supply of extra horses, filed out from among the woods and went slowly northward.

"I kind o' wish we were all back at the Alamo," remarked Joe.

"We won't go in that direction jest yit," said Jim Cheyne. "We'd better ride clean across the continent."

"Halt!" sprang from the lips of Colonel Bowie. "Here he comes! My God, boys! What's happened?"

Not with his usual swiftly gliding step, but staggering and panting as if in pain, the old Tlascalan appeared at a little distance ahead of them. He was alone, and he motioned to them to stay where they were.

"Find Comanche," suggested Red Wolf.

Bowie was silent, but when the old man drew near enough he asked,—

"Did you sight the Lipans?"

"All gone!" gasped Tetzcatl.

"Castro?"

"Gone!" came faintly back. "Great Bear's whole band. My mule! We must push on! They are crossing the Rio!"

Bowie sprang to the ground and strode forward.

"Man alive!" he said. "Where are you hurt? Tell us the rest of it while I fix you up. Jim, get that plaster and scissors out of my saddle-bags. We mustn't lose him just now."

Off came the *serape* from the old man's shoulders and an awful gash was discovered. His left arm told of an arrow, and there was a deep cut on his head. He was tough indeed to have carried all those hurts with him across the Rio Grande.

"I'm surgeon enough," remarked the colonel. "I don't believe he can live, boys, but we must do the best we can. Put him on his mule."

The wounds had been dressed with much care and skill, but the wounded man had hardly seemed to think of them. Briefly and clearly he told of his scouting beyond the river; of a meeting with Castro and then with the party of Lipans. There had been an attempt to rejoin the Texans, but in making it the entire force of Great Bear, called out by the return of the horse-thieves from the hacienda, had suddenly swarmed around them. Tetzcatl had escaped mainly because he was on foot, but a lance-thrust in the dark and the arrows that fell like snow had done their work

upon him. Here he was now, to say as persistently as ever,—

"Gold! The treasure of Montezuma."

"What do we care for gold just now?"
grumbled Jim Cheyne. "I'm thinkin' of the
ha'r on my head."

Tetzcatl raised his uninjured arm, as he
sat upon his mule, and pointed toward the
hacienda.

"Bravo's lancers," he said, "sweeping the
whole country."

"Fact!" said Jim, but Tetzcatl now pointed
northward.

"Great Bear and his Comanches all the way
to the Alamo."

"That's about so," came from one of the
rangers. "We can't git through 'em."

Once more Tetzcatl turned, and now he
pointed westward.

"Apaches!" he said. "Bowie must come
with me. A few days' ride. Then he will
come back with his ponies loaded."

He spoke with some difficulty, and at the
end of his very pointed remarks he spurred his
mule, as if he were going his own way whether
or not the Texans were to follow.

"Boys," said Bowie, "what do you say?"

"Thar isn't a word to say," growled Joe. "We've jest got to git. Come on, fellers. This crowd's travellin', gold or no gold."

"The coast 'll be clear by the time we want to come back," said the colonel. "We shall hardly meet an enemy going or coming."

So they turned and rode on after the old Tlascalan. Behind them quietly followed the Lipan boy. His young face was clouded with sorrow, but the only words that escaped him were,—

"Castro! Great chief of the Lipans! Gone! Red Wolf will strike the Comanches!"

12

CHAPTER XIII

A WEEK had gone by and a little cavalcade rode slowly on along a fairly well
marked forest road. In front was a man on a
fine-looking horse, but at his side a mule was
carrying a rider who almost lay down, with his
arms around the animal's neck.

"Can you stand it to get there?" asked the
man on the horse.

"Bowie, you are in the valley now," was the
faint-voiced response. "Ride on, Tetzcatl cannot die but in the house of Huitzilopochtli."

"Pretty nigh gone, old chap?" was the not
unkindly inquiry from the next horseman behind them. "We'll git you thar. You may
pull through. You're as tough as a hickory
knot."

They could have seen how beautiful was the
valley they were riding through if they had
not been in it. As soon, however, as the path
they were in began to climb a steep ascent and

178

they could look back through the trees, they broke out into strong expressions of admiration.

"It was a'most worth while comin'," said Jim Cheyne, "if 'twas only to see this 'ere. If Americans got hold of sech a country as this is they'd make something out of it."

"They never will," remarked Bowie. "Best timber. Best farm land in the world. Fine climate——"

"Gold! gold! Silver!" gasped the sufferer on the mule. "Americans—all men will come some day. I die, but the lands of the Montezumas will not be held by the Spaniards."

It was as if he could bear the idea of leaving his mountains and valleys and their riches to any other race than the one which had broken the empire of its ancient kings and destroyed the temples of the Aztec gods.

The Texans could also see more clearly now the grand height of the mountain chain into which they were climbing. They were evidently in a pass, partly natural and partly artificial. In places which would otherwise have been difficult the narrow roadway had been solidly constructed of massive stonework, for the greater part unhewn. There had been excavations also, but before long Joe was justified in remarking,—

"I say, colonel, this might do for mules, but it won't for mustangs. I'd ruther go afoot."

He sprang to the ground as he spoke, and his comrades followed his example. Well they might, for at their right arose an almost perpendicular cliff, while at their left the side of the mountain went down, for hundreds of feet, without a tree or a bush to prevent man or horse from rolling the entire descent.

"How far have we now to go?" asked Bowie of his guide. "Red Wolf, hold on."

"Red Wolf find road," came back in Lipan-Spanish. "Big Knife bring old man. Tetzcatl heap dead."

"Pitch ahead, then!" exclaimed the colonel. "Boys, wait here with the critters. I'll go on and find the place. The boy can come back after you."

"All right, colonel," replied Jim. "He won't last long now."

"On! on!" exclaimed Tetzcatl, his fierce, black eyes burning with the fire of the fever which had set in upon him, caused by his hurts.

"We are at the door! I will die in the house!"

He was very weak and in pain, but at the end of a hundred yards more of that steep and dangerous pass he halted his mule, slipped off to the ground, and actually stood erect.

"Stay here," he said. "No Spaniard ever entered the last house of Huitzilopochtli. I go on!"

He turned, bracing himself with all his remaining strength, and went forward as if he believed that his injunctions had been obeyed.

"Fever crazy," said the colonel, in a low voice. "Keep just behind him. If we can follow without his knowing."

That was by no means difficult, for he did not turn his head, and there were many bushes, but it was best to let him keep a number of paces in the advance.

It was a winding pathway as well as steep. There were sudden turns around rocky projections, and now the gorge at the left was deeper and more terrible to look down into.

"What?" exclaimed Bowie, as he and his boy companion turned one of these corners.

"Where is he? Did he tumble off the path?
There isn't a trace of him!"

Vacant indeed was the narrow way before
them, but Red Wolf sprang forward. The
mountain-side above was not perpendicular at
this point and there were bushes.

"Too much heap bush," said Red Wolf.
"Track rabbit into hole. Ugh!"

He parted the luxuriant growth as he spoke
and uncovered something plainer than a rabbit-
track.

"Go ahead!" said the colonel. "Don't
make a sound. He was trying to get away.
He never meant to show it to us at all. Thunder! A man might hunt for this a hundred
years and never find it."

"Ugh!" came warningly from Red Wolf, for
right before him was the cleft in the rock.

No guard was there to hinder them, but
they pushed forward with all caution. Tetzcatl
could not be many paces farther on. He must,
as yet, be entirely unaware that he had been
so closely followed.

"It's a hole into a den," muttered Bowie.
"We've got to all but go on all-fours."

It was an exciting moment with so much

mystery and uncertainty just ahead of him, but he did not betray any excitement. Hardly as much could be said for the Red Wolf, for he was on an entirely new kind of hunt and it did excite him.

There is a singular muscular power that often comes with the delirium of fever. It sometimes even exceeds, for a moment, the utmost strength of health.

Not at all feeble, but firm and elastic, was the step with which Tetzcatl walked out from the entrance burrow into the great hall of the cavern. He went forward without a pause at first, and without speaking, although something more than ordinary was going on.

The sculptured head of the war-god stood out in full relief from the dark face of the rock, for a great glare fell upon it from the altar. The fire was blazing high, revealing here and there the ghastly, ghostly figures of the priestly worshippers. They seemed to be more in number than on the day of his departure, but there were also other human beings present. Several of these latter stood immediately in front of the altar with rope fetters on their wrists.

A species of monotonous chant was sounding, by discordant voices, in the tongue of the ancient race. Every now and then, as the weird, hoarse cadences rose and fell, a club was lifted, a heavy blow was struck, followed by a flash of steel and the fall of one of the fettered persons. Each shriek of fear or agony seemed to act as a signal for louder chanting, that had in it a sound of angry mockery.

"God in heaven!" exclaimed Bowie, in a hushed whisper, at the upper end of the cave. "I've heard of it! I've read of it! That's an idol. They are offering human sacrifices. It's awful, and I can't do one thing for 'em. There went the last of 'em, as far as I can see. Red Wolf, keep close by me. I'm going to see this thing clean through. There goes Tetzcatl."

"Ugh!" was all the reply of Red Wolf, but he was apparently quite ready to charge forward, lance in hand, if such were his orders from his white chief.

Bowie had drawn his knife and had taken a heavy belt-pistol in his left hand, cocking it. He had not halted for an instant, and he was now half-way down the cavern. Here, however, he almost lay down, with Red Wolf at

his side, in so deep a shadow that there was
little danger of their presence being speedily
discovered. At that moment, moreover, the
cave-dwellers were giving all their attention to
Tetzcatl, as he stood haranguing them at the
highest pitch of his sepulchral voice. If he
were giving them an account of his journey
into Texas, only those who understood his dialect could tell, and before long he turned and
walked away toward the lower end of the cave,
still talking and gesticulating fiercely. All
the others moved when he did, and they were
dragging with them the lifeless forms of the
victims that had been slain in front of the
altar.

"This is a terrible piece of work," muttered
Bowie to himself. "I'd like to kill every one
of those fellows. I knew they were still doing
this kind of thing in Africa, wholesale and re-
tail, thousands on thousands, all the while, but
I'd reckoned it was long ago played out on this
continent. There are loads of things that we
don't know. Anyhow, this must be about the
last of it."

Not even Africa itself exceeded some parts
of America in the bloody nature of their old-

time idol-worship.   There could be, moreover, no sound reason for supposing that altogether unreclaimed heathen, here or there, would change their ways or cease from observing their rites merely because other men had become civilized.

Tetzcatl and his companions reached the level at the brink of the chasm, and the booming sound came loudly up.

"What can it be?" thought Bowie. "I'll see what they're going to do, cost what it may. There isn't a shooting-iron among 'em. Some of 'em are stark naked. If it's got to be a fight, I believe I could wipe out the whole crowd, but I don't mean to run any risks. What I want is to learn all I can this trip and get out alive."

Red Wolf went forward at his side, lance in hand, with the crouching, springing step of a young panther rather than the gliding of a wolf.

"Big Knife strike!" he said. "Heap kill. Ugh! Red Wolf! Son of Castro!"

The chanting began again, and Tetzcatl seemed to be leading it, gesticulating furiously, while body after body was lifted from the floor and hurled into the chasm to go down to the gods. As the last offering disappeared, he turned and pointed at the planks. In an instant these were raised and slipped across the chasm.

"Bridge," muttered Bowie. "I've been in caves before, but this is a pretty big one. There's more of it, I suppose, away in yonder. Best kind of hiding-place. Now, what are they going to do?"

Up to this moment Tetzcatl had exhibited the strength of the hot fever which was consuming him. Now, however, he tottered and reeled as he walked out to the middle of the bridge. Standing here, staggering back and forth, he shouted a few words in his own tongue and then plunged down, head foremost.

"That's the last of him!" exclaimed Bowie.

"Ugh!" whispered Red Wolf. "Heap look!"

The chanting began again, as if a sacrifice had been offered. One after another the withered guardians of the cave of Huitzilopochtli walked slowly across the bridge, and their torches speedily disappeared in a vast and vaulted gloom upon the other side.

" Now !" exclaimed Bowie.

He sprang to the altar and snatched from it a branch of blazing pine. Red Wolf did the same, and they were without other company when they stood together at the brink of the chasm.

" We won't go across," said Bowie; "but what's this? God in heaven! It's the treasure !"

There they lay, the stacks of ingots and the heaps of nuggets. He could not even roughly estimate their value, but he exclaimed,—

" Enough to pay the entire debt of Texas ; equip an army ; build a navy ; buy out Mexico from all the land, west, to the Pacific."

It was the golden dream of a new empire, and he stood as still as a statue for a half-minute, dreaming it, while Red Wolf lifted his torch and peered into the yawning gulf and across the bridge.

" Just as old Tetzcatl said," remarked Bowie, when his thoughtful fit ended. " But we can't take it now. There may be a hundred men in yonder. What's more, if we tried it on we might be caught in the pass by a swarm of 'em. It won't do. There are not enough of us this time. We'll have to come again. I'll take along some samples, but gold is heavy."

He began at once to cut off long strips from the *serape* which Tetzcatl had thrown upon the floor. They answered for straps with which to tie up for himself and Red Wolf as many gold bars as they could conveniently carry. They worked rapidly, for time might be precious. Not merely for the present matter of their own life or death, but that no returning idol-worshipper might know that the secret of the cavern had been discovered.

"Out now," said Bowie. "This is all we can do this time, but I don't want to see any more high old Mexican religion."

"Ugh!" said Red Wolf. "Tetzcatl gone. Heap fool jump!"

"Well," replied Bowie, coolly, "the old rascal was about dead anyhow."

After that he was silent and so was his companion, while they hurried out of the cave. They hardly uttered a word until they stood among their comrades in the pass.

"Hurrah!" shouted Jim Cheyne. "We've been up and we've been down huntin' ye. What kept ye so long, colonel?"

The fagots of golden bars were held up before the astonished eyes of the rangers, and they crowded around to see and to feel the wonderful yellow metal.

"Colonel," gasped Joe, "I don't believe a word of it, but just tell us what it is."

"The Montezuma treasure!" shouted Bowie. "Heaps on heaps of it in the cave."

"We'll go right in," responded voice after voice, in feverish eagerness.

"Not to-day, we won't," he said, and then, while they listened in awe-struck silence, he told them all there was to tell and what he intended doing.

"Your head's level," said Jim, at the conclusion of it. "We mustn't go in. We'd be followed by an army of 'em all the way to the Rio. Not one of us 'd git thar."

"Just so," said the colonel. "Now I'll swear you all in to keep the secret, and then we must be moving. We can come back with three hundred men, and even then nobody must know we're coming till the job's done clean."

Every man was ready to be sworn to secrecy, but the Texan patriot made them swear to one thing more. One full half of all that might be recovered from the cave, over and above the expenses of an expedition to obtain it, was to go into the treasury of Texas, to be spent in fighting for its freedom. They were of one accord as to that, without a dissenting voice, but Bowie was a liberal man as well as patriotic and prudent, and as soon as the future was duly cared for, he saw that it was right and wise to provide them with a sufficient reward for their services in the present expedition.

" You've done well this first time," had come from Jim Cheyne.

" Well," said the colonel, " these things are near of a size. We'll divide 'em, share and share alike, every fellow to tote his own winnings. It 'll be the best four weeks' work any of you were ever paid for——"

" Half to Texas anyhow!" shouted Jim, as he handled the bars that fell to his lot. " The republic can have my whole pile if I'm knocked on the head. Hurrah! Now for home! We've done enough!"

As for Red Wolf, he hardly knew what to do with three long, heavy, dingy sticks of metal that were assigned to him. He fastened them behind the saddle which now adorned his mustang, but he did so out of respect for Big Knife. The saddle itself was a kind of pale-face emcumbrance, but he had won it at the hacienda, and he rode in it for the sake of glory, as a prize of war.

As for regarding a gold bar as a silver dollar, he had not yet climbed as high as that. The nearest he came to an understanding was when Joe held up one of his own bars and shouted,—

"I say, colonel, just what we've got here would buy another eighteen-pounder as big as the one in the Alamo."

"Two of 'em," replied Bowie, "and a dozen rounds apiece of powder and ball. That's what we want,—powder and ball. Boys! One more secret! I'm going to take you right thar! We'll go home with cash enough to put the Alamo in first-rate order, rations, rifles, and all. Forward, march!"

On they went, down the mountain, carrying with them the secret of the treasures of the Montezumas.

CHAPTER XIV

CAN the mere possession of a secret turn a brave man into a coward? One would think not, and yet the entire demeanor and conduct of Colonel Bowie underwent a change. It seemed to be growing upon him, as he led the way down the pass and out into the valley. His men, too, hardened frontiersmen and Indian fighters as they were, responded almost nervously to his every suggestion of extreme watchfulness.

There were good reasons for it all. They had reached the valley in peace, but no one could guess by what eyes their arrival had been noted, or what forces might be gathering to strike a blow at them.

The dark clans of the Mexican mountains were known to be courageous. No other men had a greater disregard for either the lives of other men or their own. They had succeeded in protecting their fastnesses so perfectly that

the Spanish and then the several Mexican gov-
ernments had consented to let them alone. As
to the latter, indeed, the short history of Mexico as an independent state had been, thus far,
little better than the record of struggles for
power between warring chiefs and factions.
Whoever at any date had been temporarily
in authority had had quite enough to do to
maintain his own supremacy. There had been
few troops to spare for operations against the
red men of the North, and none at all for the
penetration of the really undiscovered country
which contained such remnants as Tetzcatl and
his comrades of the cave.

"They could wipe us out, boys," was the
freely expressed opinion all around, and they
were ready, as Joe expressed it, " to just sneak
all the way back, if we've any idee of comin'
this way ag'in after that pewter."

Bowie's own calculations continually went
on beyond the dangers of the road.

" I've got to reach Houston," he said, "and
set him at work with those dollars. We can
make up a force to come again with. I can trust
Crockett and Travis. We can have our pick
of men. But we needn't let the rank and file

know the whole thing. One of 'em might let it out too soon. If we work still enough, we can ride across all this country and hardly stir up the Mexicans. One big mule train 'll carry all there is in the cave. We can get it across the Rio Grande, perhaps, without having to fire a shot. Not that I mind fighting, if it comes to that, but as soon as it's all landed as far as the Alamo, the republic of Texas is a made nation. We can arm all the men we can raise, and we can whip Santa Anna out of his boots."

It was the fate of the future that was in his mind and on his shoulders. If he should now get himself killed, with his little band of rangers, who would ever know where to come for the treasures of the Montezumas?

As for Red Wolf, the secret did not trouble him. It did not seem to belong to him at all. Nevertheless, it was entirely in accord with his ideas that a war-party, returning through an enemy's country, should travel as stealthily as so many wild animals.

That first night no fire was kindled, and the march began again before the sun was up. Before the end of the next day one worn-out horse had to be left behind.

"We'll use 'em all up if need be," remarked Bowie. "All I want is to get to the chaparral with critters enough to go home from there on a walk."

It was on one of those days of watchful, tiresome pushing for the men who had the secret to carry and the ingots of gold from the cave, but it was hundreds of miles away from them that a group of very serious-looking men sat around a table in a log farm-house. If it were any kind of council, the conversational part of it had momentarily ceased and they all were thinking silently.

A heavy step sounded outside the door; it swung suddenly open, and a voice not at all loud but very much in earnest startled them to their feet.

"Here I am, Houston! They're coming!"

"Crockett!" shouted the astonished general. "I thought you were in Washington."

"Well, I ain't, then," responded the grim bear-killer, throwing his coonskin cap violently upon the table. "I didn't git beyond New Orleans. I found a heap of letters thar, and thar was all sorts of deviltry in 'em. It's no use to look for anything from Congress this session, and that ain't the wust of it."

"Out with it, colonel," came from across the table. "Let's have it all. We were having a blue time anyhow."

"Stingy! stingy! stingy!" roared Crockett. "Everybody's afraid to put in a cent. Not a dollar to be had, nor any pound of stuff without the dollars. You see, boys, the trouble is the news from Mexico. Santa Anna was at Monterey gathering his best troops and getting ready to come after us. Thar are several regiments already down near Matamoras on the coast getting supplies by the sea. Every friend of ours seems to be skeered. They reckon we'll be chawed up."

"Not so easy," came again from across the table. "I reckon the Greasers have got their work cut out."

"Travis," said Crockett, "I'm glad you're here. Have you heard from Bowie?"

"Not a word," replied Travis, "except that he and Castro had some kind of a brush with the Comanches, and another with Bravo's lancers. Reckon it was all right. He's just the kind of fellow to pull through."

Even while he spoke, however, the bright-faced ranger colonel caught Crockett's eye and sent him a look that prevented further questioning.

"Time for us to be moving," said Houston, steadily. "We'll gather what forces we can. The first thing is the Alamo. We can send a pretty good lot of rations."

"Powder!" said Travis, with energy. "What the Alamo needs is powder. And we want men enough to handle guns."

"You shall have them," said Houston. "Texas won't leave you in the lurch. Go and put things in as good condition as you can."

"All right," said Travis; but Crockett was eager to learn whatever news might be had around the table, and he lingered to get it all. At last he and Travis walked out into the open air, and they were no sooner alone than the latter turned and looked his friend in the face.

"Crockett," he said, "either Bowie is wiped out, or he and his men have ridden down into Mexico after that gold of Tetzcatl's."

"That's what he's done, then," said Crockett, confidently. "He's a critter that 'll take no end of killing. He had the right sort of men with him. What I want is to see him back ag'in, gold or no gold, and to have him with us when the Greasers come for the Alamo. I mean to be thar myself."

"Crockett," replied Bowie, "Sam Houston is mistaken. He can't raise a dollar. All we've got to depend on is the men. We'll take our pick, though, and we can hold that fort against all the ragamuffins south of the Rio Grande."

On they walked, talking as they went, but if they could have had a look at some of Santa Anna's "ragamuffins" they might not have felt so confident.

In the great plaza of the city of Monterey, in front of the church, a regiment of infantry was at that hour paraded for inspection. Their arms were good, for they had just been imported from across the Atlantic. Their uniforms were new. Their drill was fair. They seemed to be well handled. They were not by any means, in appearance at least, the kind of soldiers to be despised by a half-armed garrison of an old *adobe* fort. Even the stone part of the Alamo defences might be in danger, for a battery of heavy cannon was drawn up near them. In front of the line were halted a dozen or so of officers on horseback, brilliant in equipment, whose bronzed and bearded faces wore a very warlike look.

Encamped near the city walls, outside, were other regiments and other batteries. What could the Texans mean by their contempt for the forces which were to come against them? What hope had their poverty-stricken little state in a struggle against such numbers and such resources as now were gathering to conquer it?

The review was over. A salute was fired by the battery. The troops cheered. The name of Santa Anna mingled loudly with the cheering, and the general, sending his splendid horse forward, raised his hat gracefully in response. But then he turned to his attendant officers and remarked,—

"It is well, gentlemen. The troops are in fine condition. We shall sweep the Gringos out of Texas. Now for the cock-fight, and then we will have a quiet game of monte at the palace."

He had pretty fairly condensed into his remarks one feature of the situation. The sturdy riflemen of the American border were strongly impressed with the worthlessness of the Mexican military organization; with the dissipated, lazy character of its men and their commanders; and they confidently expected that a Mexican invasion of Texas would be little more than a campaign of wasteful blunders.

"If we can stand their first rush," had been said by General Houston, "they'll break all to pieces before they make another."

If Travis and his friends were beginning to be anxious concerning the fate of Bowie, he was all the while growing more and more anxious about it himself. He would have been more so if the region of country he was pushing his way through had not been so very nearly unoccupied. Here and there a fortified town or village needed to be given a wide berth. Strongly built haciendas were to be avoided, if they were not already deserted. Most of them were so by reason of the recent civil wars, and yet more on account of the destructive raids of the red men. It was a nearly ruined country, and it was not altogether impossible for even a considerable band of prudent men to travel across it without attracting too much attention.

The men discussed the probabilities again and again, and their leader was studying them carefully, but from time to time he shook his head.

"Boys," he remarked, as they sat around their camp-fire in the woods that evening, "you're only half right. We could march an expedition along by this route and not find a soul to hinder us, but there'd be a whole brigade of lancers riding this way before we could get the bullion and set out for home. I reckon they'd meet us somewhere about here. They could pen us in."

"Colonel," replied Jim Cheyne, "I've thought of that. This is the shortest road to come or go on, isn't it?"

"By all odds the shortest," said Bowie.

"Then it's our road to come back, and we can choose a roundabout road to go there by. They'll foller our trail, and we kin make one we'd jest as lieve they would foller. We kin beat 'em."

It was a kind of relief to their present anxiety to sit there and make plans for the future. They were never tired, moreover, of hearing again and again a description of the cavern, the idol, the sacrifices, the plunges into the chasm, and the heaps of gold and silver. Some day they were to see it all for themselves, and they were to take the treasure out of the cave and pack it upon their mules and ponies. Then they were to go home with it. They could buy plantations, build houses, "live like gentlemen," as Joe was fond of saying, and all the while they could strengthen Texas and help its riflemen to drive out Santa Anna.

One of their number, however, did not care a button for anything that they were saying. Not any of it belonged to him. All that he knew about was the present, and all that he could feel were his keen instincts as a young Lipan warrior with a party of white men upon his hands. They were friends of his, and it was his duty to take care of them. He had gone to sleep at once that evening, after eating his supper at sunset, but not long after the weary rangers spread their blankets and lay down their very red associate was up again.

Joe was acting as sentry at the foot of a tree, with his rifle across his lap, but he paid no attention to Red Wolf when he saw him walking toward the nearest underbrush.

"Indian!" he muttered. "Let him rip."

"Red Wolf heap look," said he, a few minutes afterwards, as he came out into a place
where the trees were widely scattered.

A white man might not have seen anything,
for all around him was as dark as a pocket, but
upon a cloudy gloom above the forest beyond
him there rested a faint, yellowish glow.

"Ugh!" he exclaimed. "Fire burn."

He had brought no weapons with him
excepting the knife and pistols in his belt,
but he was now armed better than were most
Indian boys, and Bowie had promised him a
rifle.

From tree to tree, keeping among the
shadows, on he went, and all the while the
glow grew brighter, until at last he could see
the flashing of fires and the forms of those
around them.

"Ugh!" said Red Wolf. " Mexican. No
Comanche. Heap sleep."

In every direction lay the prostrate forms of
men. Standing erect or walking hither and
thither were a few who might be acting as a
night watch. A group of these were gathered
at the end of the camp nearest the young scout

or spy, and he crept toward them, for they were jabbering loudly in Spanish. They carried weapons, bows and arrows, *escopetas*, or short muskets, *machetes* of all sorts and sizes, knives, lances, hatchets, clubs. They were not regular soldiers, but their numbers made them sufficiently dangerous.

" Eat up Texan," thought Red Wolf. " No catch him. Go back."

He went rapidly enough, until Joe, at the foot of his tree, was startled by a hand upon his shoulder. A few swift words told him what was the matter, and the other rangers were at once roughly stirred up.

" Do you s'pose, colonel," asked Cheyne, " that we've been followed ?"

" Not a bit of it !" exclaimed Bowie. " These chaps got their cue from Tetzcatl somehow while we were on the way. He never meant we should find out this thing and get home again. They don't know the secret either. All they know is that we're a squad of Gringos, and that we must be chopped up. Most likely they heard of us to-day, and mean to strike us in the morning. We must git ! That's all."

" Bully for Red Wolf !" seemed to express

the general opinion of the rangers, but the half-rested, half-fed animals were untethered at once.

"If it hadn't been for you they'd ha' corralled us," remarked Cheyne to Red Wolf, but all the response he obtained was "Ugh!"

"We have everything in our favor," said the colonel, "now we've passed 'em. Such a crowd as that won't stir out early. They'll all lie around and jabber and smoke cigarettes and drink pulque and gamble and boast, and then they'll swarm in to find that we've stolen a march on 'em."

For once he was mistaken in his estimate of his enemies. It was in the very dawn of the day, when he and his comrades might have been supposed to be asleep, that the miscellaneous militia from the Mexican camp "swarmed in" to slaughter the too adventurous Gringos. It was a sudden rush, made at a signal, a musket-shot, and it was made with wild shouts of anticipated triumph. It would have been entirely successful but for the fact that Bowie and his men had been pushing northward during four long hours, at a rate which had compelled them to abandon one more of their over-driven horses.

" We've learned one lesson," said the colonel, when at last they halted on the northerly bank of a stream which had proved barely fordable. " When we come again we can make sure that all the Greasers will gather behind us to cut off our retreat."

" That's what I was saying," replied Cheyne. " We mustn't try to go and come by the same road."

" Ugh!" said Red Wolf. " Bring heap Texan. Mexican run."

" There's a good deal in that," laughed Bowie, " but we don't want to have to fight at all. We must work it as sly as so many horse-thieves. We shall be carrying too much plunder to want a battle with Bravo's lancers."

They were safe for the present, however, and after only a brief rest they went on again—for life.

CHAPTER XV.

" WELL, boys, we got in like woodchucks by the same hole we came out of," said Colonel Bowie to his men.

" Reckon the lancers are scouting the south prairie after us yet," replied Jim Cheyne.

" They didn't knew about the ravine, Jim," said another ranger. " But ain't I glad we're safe in among the bushes."

Here they were, at all events, plodding along one of the sandy avenues of the chaparral. Both the men and their horses had a worn and jaded look.

" Our tramp's nearly ended," continued the colonel. " The lancers made it a close shave from the Rio Grande to the Nueces, but we've beaten 'em. We know now that Santa Anna is in Texas, and we're back in time to take our part in the fight. We've had good weather to travel in, but so will he. It's getting on into the spring."

208

"Ugh!" exclaimed Red Wolf, pausing before a tree. "Heap Comanche in bushes. Great Bear sign."

There was a gash upon the tree, such as might be made with a knife. It was a curved line with a notch in the middle, for a bow with an arrow, it might be.

"Made to-day," said Bowie, as he studied the mark. "The sap is running. We'll have to keep a sharp lookout if we mean to get through, but they can't know we're here."

It was a warning of an unexpected danger, but it did not seem to depress them. On the contrary, their faces were bright and hopeful, in spite of the fact that they had left so many tired-out horses by the way that they now had only one mount left for each man.

"We haven't lost a man," remarked Jim, cheerfully, "and we've kept every pound of the rhino. We're going back after the rest of it, too."

"We are!" said Bowie, with almost an appearance of enthusiasm. "We'll set out as soon as Texas is clear of Santa Anna."

"That's it," said Joe; "but you see, as soon as he's well whipped the coast 'll be clearer than it ever was before."

14

On they pushed, and Red Wolf rode in the advance as a kind of guide. Part of the time he was hidden from his white friends by the crooks and turns of the path by which he was leading them, and now and then he had to ride back to indicate the right way.

"It takes a redskin," they said more than once, "and he's jest the reddest Indian there ever was."

That was so, for the sun had not appeared to have any power over the peculiar tint of his skin, but all the while he had seemed to be growing older. If he had been a boy when he joined them at the Alamo, Red Wolf was now a warrior, tested by the emergencies of a very uncommon "war-path."

The hours went swiftly by and there was no haste to be made.

"Go slow," had been the repeated injunction of Bowie. "The main thing is to get there."

It must have been about noon when Red Wolf came riding back with a hand lifted in warning.

"What is it?" asked Bowie.

"Ugh!" he said. "Great Bear in bushes. Heap Comanche. Big Knife heap snake."

He wheeled his mustang to the right and they followed him.

"It's awful!" exclaimed Cheyne. "Colonel, the Comanches have joined the Mexicans. What about the Lipans?"

"Fighting the Comanches," responded Bowie. "The trouble is that they seem to be expecting us. If we can ride around 'em, though, we'll get in."

"All right," said Jim, "but things are looking a little squally. I'd like to give 'em a shot or two."

"Not a shot if we can help it," said Bowie. "Wait till I show you something. It's only a short ride now."

It was much longer because of the detour, and Red Wolf was now once more out of sight.

"What's that?" exclaimed Bowie. "What on earth made him whoop? They've got him! Gallop, men! Save him if we can!"

They went forward at a swifter gait, but there was no saving to be done. They were already nearer than they had supposed to the pond and the ruins. The young Lipan had pressed on also, with a pretty clear idea in his head. He had even ridden to the border of the open, and had been looking out and around it searchingly.

"Ugh!" he said, "Great Bear no come!"

"Ugh!" exclaimed a deep voice from a thicket near him. "Castro!"

"Whoo-oo-oop!" burst from the lips of Red Wolf, and he wheeled his pony right into the thicket. "Castro!"

He could not have held in that burst of surprise and joy, nor could the chief himself have done otherwise than to come out from his hiding-place with a great bound. Swift, indeed, were the explanations which were exchanged. Only a brief outline could be given by Red Wolf of his wonderful campaign in Mexico. The particulars would have to wait. Castro himself could do but little better at that moment.

"Tetzcatl heap liar!" contained the root of the matter.

He had said very little more than that when they heard hushed voices in the pathway near them.

"Jest about yer it was," said one.

"Look out sharp now!" said another.

"I'll find his carkiss if I can," came from

Joe. "He was a buster. But what did he whoop for?"

"He ort not to," remarked Jim, "but I s'pose he couldn't. help it. Now they'll all know we've come. But I just liked that young feller."

"Ugh!" said Castro. "Heap friend of Red Wolf. Boy talk."

Out darted Red Wolf, and in a moment more there were hearty hand-shakings all around.

Castro had ghastly tokens to show of the blows he had stricken upon his Comanche enemies, but now he gave also a better account of the manner of his separation from his friends on the night after they went over the Rio Grande.

There had been, as Tetzcatl had reported, a sharp brush between the Lipans and a party of Comanches. The old Tlascalan had only overstated the affair in order that he might carry off the Texans with him.

"All gone" had been partly true, nevertheless, for the Lipans, losing a few braves, had been forced to retreat toward the north. They had thereby been compelled to give up any idea of trying to join Bowie's party.

Ever since then, believing that his son and his friends had been " wiped out," the revengeful chief had been hanging upon the movements of Great Bear's band wherever they went or came. He was now informed somewhat more fully of what the adventurers had been doing, but it was no time for too much talk.

" Forward now," exclaimed Bowie, at last. " Our next business is to get the cash and push on to the Alamo. We're pretty nigh out of powder ourselves. We couldn't stand a long fight."

On they went, therefore, cautiously enough, but when they reached the open it seemed entirely deserted. They halted in the bushes while Castro and Red Wolf made circuits to the right and left.

" Men," said Bowie, with emphasis, while they waited, " we'll go in and get it. We must take almost any risk to carry it off. But don't you forget, if I go down, that this cash belongs to Texas. 'Tisn't yours nor mine, except each man's fair allowance for taking it in. None of you fellows found it, in the first place."

"All right, colonel," responded Joe. "Hurrah for Texas. I don't want any dollar that isn't mine."

"Don't hurrah quite yet," said Bowie. "We don't know how near we may be to a hundred scalping-knives. Hullo! Here they come."

It was the two Lipans and not the Comanches that he referred to.

"Big Knife walk along," said Castro, as he came nearer. "No Comanche."

"I'd like to give 'em a hit," growled Bowie, "but this isn't the time for it. Come on, boys. We mustn't waste a minute."

Even now he seemed perfectly cool, but none of the other Texans failed to show how strongly the "hidden treasure" fever had taken hold of them. It grew manifestly hotter after they had ridden to the ruined *adobe* house, dismounted, and followed their leader in. It was almost impossible to believe that he was about to show them anything like actual gold and silver.

"You don't mean to say," said Joe, "that such a feller as old Tetzcatl left anything behind him up here?"

"No, he didn't," replied Bowie. "This isn't any Montezuma money. My notion is that it's old Spanish funds. If so, all the more does it of right belong now to the State of Texas."

"Of course it does!" said Cheyne, and the others heartily echoed him.

"Out it comes, then!" shouted the colonel, with the first external flash of the excitement which had all the while been smouldering within him. "You'll see what it is now. You didn't more'n half believe me, did you? Look at that!"

Over rolled the *adobe* fragments which concealed the cash, and out came bag after bag, cast down with a chink to be at once caught up by eager hands and opened. It was a breathless kind of work to make those bags tell what was in them.

"It's a pity so much of it's only silver," remarked Jim, regretfully; "but silver's better'n nothin'."

"Every feller wants more than he's got," said Joe, "but you'd kinder ought to be satisfied this time."

Red Wolf and his father had looked on in

silence, but now the chief beckoned to his son and walked out.

"Ugh!" he said. "Red Wolf tell story. Talk Mexico. Long trail? Heap fight?"

All that remained to be told of the trip with Tetzcatl came out rapidly, until the mountain pass was reached and the doings in the cavern.

"Ugh!" sharply exclaimed Castro. "Shut mouth! Montezuma bad medicine! Texan all die. Big Knife go under. Red Wolf? No! Red Wolf Indian. No hurt him. Lose hair if he talk."

He said more, but his entire meaning seemed to be that it was a well-understood doctrine that any white adventurer learning the secrets of the Aztec gods was a doomed man. They would surely follow him up and kill him. It was not so bad for a full-blooded Indian, but even a Lipan would do well to forget anything he had heard or seen that belonged to the bloody mysteries of the evil "manitous" of the old race. It was evidently a deeply rooted superstition, and Red Wolf was quite ready to accept it fully. They returned to the ruin in time to hear Bowie remark,—

"Two hundred thousand, pretty nigh, dollars

and doubloons.   Now, boys, a thousand apiece for taking it in.   All the rest goes to fight Santa Anna."

"That's the talk!" said the rangers, and the horses were led up to receive their loads.

It was not very easy to pack the ponderous stuff, even at the sacrifice of all the blankets on hand.   After it was done, moreover, another fact was evident.

"Boys," said Joe, "it's a walk for us all the way to the Alamo."

"That 'll just suit the critters," replied the colonel.   "It's all the're fit for.   But we mustn't fail to get there.   I kind o' feel as if Texas was getting safer."

They were themselves by no means safe and it was time to go forward.   The horses had picked a little grass.   They had been watered, and so had the feverish, anxious rangers, but rest for either was not to be thought of.

Slowly, cautiously, the devious avenues of the seemingly endless thickets were traversed, and at last the little calvacade, with its precious freight, emerged among the scattered trees on the border of the prairie.

" 'Tisn't time for us to whistle yet," said

Bowie, "even if we're out o' the woods. Hullo! Men! There they come! Forward! Double lines. Horses outside."

"Whoop! Whoop!" came fiercely from Castro and his son.

"I reckon we've been watched for somehow," growled Jim. "We'll show 'em a good fight for the pewter, but don't I wish thar was more of us!"

It seemed as if the loads of dollars added to the desperate courage of the men, and they made ready for the coming fight as if more than their own lives were depending upon it.

The horses were ranged in parallel lines, and the riflemen walked on in the space between. It was a kind of travelling breastwork, and it must have had a dangerous look to an outsider. A number of wild horsemen, therefore, contented themselves, for the present, with whooping loudly and riding around at safe distances. There were a great many of them, but Castro declared that the entire force under Great Bear had not made its appearance.

"It looks bad for our side," said Bowie. "It's a long time since any Comanche war-parties have ventured in as far as they have this season. Santa Anna was quite enough for us to handle without the redskins."

He hardly knew, at that moment, how dark a cloud seemed to be hanging over Texas in those closing days of the winter of 1835–1836. All things had been going wrong. There were quarrels among leaders, and even Houston had lost, apparently, a great deal of his popularity. As Crockett expressed it,—

"The cusses expect the old man to do some things that can't be did."

There were a great many things that he could not do. Nevertheless, he worked unceasingly. He made visits of inspection here and there. He made speeches, printed patriotic appeals in the newspapers, and argued with timid or disaffected settlers.

It all seemed to be of little use. The Indians were busy on the borders. Reports of the feeling in the Congress of the United States were discouraging. All the while, moreover, every arrival from south of the Rio Grande told of the extensive preparations which the Mexican president was making for an invasion. He was said to have gathered a force that would prove overwhelming, and he had declared death to all rebels.

"If we don't look out," said Crockett to Travis that afternoon, as they stood together in the open gate-way of the Alamo, "the Greasers 'll catch us all in bed. But don't I wish I knew what had become of Bowie and his men?"

"They won't fetch back any gold," replied Travis; "but I'd like to see them if they rode in as bare as redskins."

"Colonel," exclaimed Crockett, "give me a dozen men and let me take a scout over the south prairie. I might have some kind o' luck. Might knock over a Comanche."

"Let you have 'em?" said Travis, with sudden energy. "Take 'em! I'll come right along with you. I'm dog tired of loafing in this coop. Get your men."

The rangers of the garrison were as weary of inaction as was their commander, and double the number called for almost insisted upon mounting for the proposed scout.

"The fort 'll keep till we git back," remarked Crockett; "but if I don't git out of it and shoot something I shall spile."

There were very good military reasons for precisely such an errand of inquiry. The vicinity of prowling savages was pretty well known, and it was desirable to learn as much more as possible.

The party from the fort rode out, therefore, and they were well upon their way, but they were not near enough to hear the whoops of Great Bear's warriors nor the cracking of the first rifles which replied.

There had been a steady onward march of Bowie's men, without any other change in the situation than an increase in the number of their enemies.

"Boys," the colonel said, "we've gained about a mile and a half, but they're closing in on us a little. Let 'em have a pill first chance you get. Halt!"

There they stood, their rifles levelled across the saddles. It was hardly worth while to waste their small stock of powder upon swiftly careering horsemen, although now these were frequently within range.

"I'll take that drove," exclaimed Jim, as several of the whoopers wheeled into a closely gathered group.

"Got him!" he shouted, as his rifle cracked.

"One more," added Bowie. "Hold your fire, men. It won't do to have too many guns empty at one time."

The backs of two mustangs were empty, however, and the yells which followed were those of angry braves who had been stung to rashness rather than intimidated. Of course, they all wheeled away at first, taking their dead comrades with them.

The Texans again moved steadily forward, but hardly more than a quarter of a mile had been gained before Bowie shouted,—

"Here they are, men! The whole band has got in on us this time. They're gathering for a rush. Ready! Die game!"

A swarm,—a cloud,—an overwhelming torrent of the fierce cavalry of the plains, was forming in loose but effective array to sweep in upon their victims. What could six rifles and two bows do against such a storm as was now about to burst?

"Die like men!" shouted Bowie. "Kill every redskin you can draw a bead on!"

Crack, crack, went rifle after rifle, and not a shot was thrown away; but the Comanches were whooping forward upon their charge and all would soon be over.

"Hullo! What's that?" shouted the colonel.

"Whoop!" yelled Castro. "Rifle!"

"Ugh!" said Red Wolf. "Heap Texan! Comanche lose hair!"

Sharp, rapid, utterly unexpected, was the rattle of rifle-shots from away beyond the cloud of pony riders. Down went horse and man in quick succession.

"Travis and the rangers!" yelled Jim Cheyne.

"The boys have come! Thank God!" gasped Bowie. "Five minutes more and Houston wouldn't have had a dollar of this stuff."

Not even then was he wasting a thought upon his own life or upon the lives of those who were with him.

It was a terrific surprise to the red riders. They were smitten as by lightning. They could have no idea of the numbers of their new assailants, and they were in wholesome dread of the markmanship of the Texans. Well they might be!

Wheeling into a line at the order of their

commander, the rangers were deliberately picking off warrior after warrior until their rifles were empty.

"Forward! Charge!" shouted Travis.

"Come on, fellers!" yelled Crockett. "It's Bowie and the boys! Don't you miss a shot."

They were not missing so long as any human target was within pistol range, but the targets were getting away. This was not at all what they had counted on. They fought for a moment, of course, for they were warriors, and their flights of arrows were not sent in vain.

Right through them rode the rangers, leaving three of their number on the grass, while several more carried with them well-aimed arrows.

"Hot work," laughed Travis, "but here we are! Bowie, old fellow! Hurrah!"

Away wheeled the stricken Comanches, for the rangers were reloading. The savage rush was over and the next business was to get out of rifle range.

It was a curious spectacle. There stood Crockett, the rough old bear hunter, the sarcastic humorist, the lank, lantern-jawed frontiersman, hugging Colonel Bowie. It almost seemed as if he were crying.

" Hurrah !" he shouted. " I kind o' knowed they hadn't wiped him out."

" Crockett, old boy !" said Travis. " Give him a chance to speak. You are choking him."

" Jest what I want to do," said Davy. " Now, Bowie, whar have you been ?"

" Let go, Crockett," said Bowie, " and I'll tell you. But some of the men are hurt——"

" The boys are 'tending to 'em," replied Travis. " How about Tetzcatl ?"

" Not a word of him now !" burst from Bowie, vehemently. " Travis! I've found cash enough to pay for all the ammunition we need to whip Mexico. I'll tell you as we go along. Where's Sam Houston ?"

" He's to be at the fort to-day," said Crockett. " But whar on earth did you pick up any dollars ?"

The first answer was Bowie's finger on his lips. Then they three mounted and rode on together.

As for the rest of the rangers, they were indeed caring for the wounded, and even for the dead, but the story of the cash found in the ruined *adobe* house was travelling fast from man to man.

That was followed, of course, by an account of the raid into Mexico with Tetzcatl, but that part of the story was defective. As it was related it did not contain any intimation of the mountain pass, the cavern, or the treasure of the Montezumas. It did not, and yet one ranger after another said to the man next him, in varied forms of speech,—

"Tell you what, those fellows that went with Bowie are keeping back something. They've learned more than they're willin' to tell. We must get it out of 'em."

As for Red Wolf, he and his father had been lost sight of for a few minutes, but in the last part of that close, terrible fight they had been plying their bows incessantly, and now they were out on the prairie. They were Indians, Lipans, an old warrior and a young brave, and they were following the custom of their race, for they were taking trophies.

CHAPTER XVI

"HOUSTON? You here? I've something to show you. Hurrah for Texas!"

The commander-in-chief had been sent for days earlier, and he had come in haste, for a fast-riding courier had brought him word that Santa Anna and his army were already across the Rio Grande.

"Bowie! Thank God!" almost roared the old hero, springing forward. "Oh, Bowie! I'd begun to believe you were dead."

"Not a bit of it!" shouted back Bowie. "I've won a pot of money for our side. Here it comes."

A train of horses was filing through the gate-way of the Alamo. They were not the worn-out animals which had travelled so fast and so far, for Crockett had made the rangers give up as many quadrupeds as were necessary for the wounded men and the money-packs. Three horses, indeed, bore sadder burdens, for the dead also had been brought in. These had halted outside the walls and a burial party was at work.

"It costs us something to win freedom," was the sombre comment of General Houston. "Many another brave fellow must go down before we clean out the Greasers and the redskins. Now, Bowie, come in and tell me what this means."

They walked on into an inner room of the fort, but not even to Houston did Bowie as yet unfold the secret of the cavern.

"Too many know it already, or half know it," was the thought he did not put into words. He told all about the Spanish dollars and doubloons, however. In turning them over to the state, less the small sums agreed upon as the allowance of his men, he stipulated that the first use made of any money should be for provisions, powder and ball, for the defence of the Alamo.

"Houston," he said, with emphasis, "my notion is that it can't get here any too quick. Travis is wrong. Santa Anna will march straight for the Alamo."

"He may. He may," replied the general. "At all events, I must set out with the cash.

I must send you all the help I can right away.
Then I must raise troops and march to meet
the Mexicans. It's a blue time for Texas, but
this is a ray of light."

It was only one ray, for in all other dirce-
tions the prospect seemed dark. His own preparations for departure were made at once, and
in the gloom of that very evening he rode away.

"We must go all night," he said, "and not
a soul outside the fort must know what we're
taking with us."

About an hour later, eleven men sat together
in the upper corner room of the convent building, and every man of them bound by an oath
and by his word of honor to keep secret all he
might hear.

"Boys," said Bowie to his own men, "if
Travis and Crockett are let in and no more,
the secret is just as safe. I don't feel as if they
were outsiders."

"Just the same as ourselves," replied Jim
Cheyne. "They're to help us git up the expedition. But what about the gold bars we
fetched this time? They'd tell it all if we
showed 'em now."

"Keep 'em for expenses when we are ready

for business," said Bowie. "I didn't say a word of them to Houston. We can hole them right here in the corner of this room. Safe as a bank."

"And if Santa Anna captures the fort, what then?" asked Joe.

"Nobody 'll ever hear of any gold he got here," replied Bowie, grimly. "If one of his men found it, he'd take it away from him and have him shot for desertion."

The bars belonging to the men were brought, and they made only a small pile, after all, when packed in a corner, under the couch, with old saddles stuffed in front of them. Red Wolf's prizes, of course, were not included.

"Ugh!" said Castro, after watching the operation. "Big Knife kill Travis. Kill Crockett. No kill all Texan. Heap shut mouth. Montezuma talk, all bad medicine."

"All right, Castro," said Bowie. "When my time comes I shall die."

"What does he mean?" asked Travis.

"You couldn't root it out of him," said Bowie. "He believes that every white man who meddles with this stuff is bound to go under. It's poison."

"Out with your yarn, then," said Crockett.

"I'll take my chances. You kin name the day for my funeral."

Steadily, from step to step, the colonel told the story of his raid into Mexico. Not a word was uttered by anybody else until he came to the description of the cavern.

"Ugh!" exclaimed Castro. "Heap bad medicine. Now Travis go under. Crockett lose hair."

He evidently did not wish to hear any more himself, but curiosity is a strong tether, and, after all, he was an Indian, and upon him the mysterious peril might not have so much power. Red Wolf knew the secret already, and nothing evil had as yet happened to him. The chief remained, therefore, in silence, while Bowie told of the human sacrifices, the fate of Tetzcatl, and the heaps of ingots, tons and tons of them.

"Go for it?" shouted Travis. "Of course we will. As soon as we've beaten the Greasers I'll raise the men that can ride across Mexico to get the stuff out of that cave. It's a wonderful thing to know, but when you come to think of it, it's the most natural thing in the world. Montezuma and Guatamoczin did exactly what you and I would have done, both before Cortez came and afterwards.   We wouldn't have given it up neither, and they didn't."

"Thar's heaps of human natur' in this world," remarked Crockett.   "I'd ha' bet they'd ha' done just exactly what they did do. There's nothing curious about it."

"No more there is about their idols," added Travis.   "They kept them just as all the other heathen do in Asia and Africa.   Hundreds of millions of idol-worshippers go it right along, with the missionaries among 'em.   They kill the missionaries, too, now and then.   Some eat 'em, and these fellows cut their throats and pitch 'em into a hole."

It seemed as if every trace of anything mysterious or improbable departed from the old legend of the Aztec gold and silver the moment the truth concerning it came out to be studied by such matter-of-fact men as these. Their hard common sense took it like any other business affair, and they were almost ready to name beforehand the men they meant to take with them on the expedition they planned to secure the treasure.

After telling the story, however, Bowie grew silent and moody.   He looked around him upon the bare walls of the room. He passed a hand over the low couch upon which he was sitting. He hardly seemed to listen to what the others were saying. When at last there was a pause and a silence, he arose to his feet, and a shadow, darker than usual, was on his face.

"Travis," he said, "I want to get out of this room. It's close and hot. I somehow don't like it. It keeps me thinking of Tetzcatl, too, and of all he said when we talked with him here. He was a kind of devil, he was. I'm glad he went down into that chasm. If it's good and deep he'll stay there."

He strode rapidly out of the room, and they heard Castro mutter,—

"Big Knife too much talk. Montezuma talk bad medicine. All lose hair. Ugh!"

Red Wolf had listened but he had said nothing, for nothing was left him to tell. He was a proud young brave, however, for the Big Knife, the great white chief, had praised him tremendously, and his own father had more than once said, "Heap young brave."

"Ugh!" said Castro, laying a hand upon the arm of his son; and they arose and followed Bowie until they stood with him in the plaza.

"Well, Castro?" asked Bowie. "What is it?"

"Want horse," said the Lipan chief. "Good pony. Ride heap. See Mexican. Come tell Bowie. Sleep now. Go before sun."

"Bully!" exclaimed Bowie. "I'll give you the best critters in the fort. I want to know just where Santa Anna is. What you two want first, though, is to sleep about ten hours and eat all you can hold."

Castro meant just that, for even the tough sinews of a Lipan warrior could feel the strain they had borne. Away he went with Red Wolf, and now the colonel's face grew brighter, for half the garrison was gathering around him.

"I can't talk much now, boys," he said. "You know about all there is to tell, but I'll add one thing."

He pointed westward in silence for a moment, and his eyes wore almost a dreamy look as he went on:

"All that land, clean through to the Pacific, must belong to Texas. Somewhere in yonder among the mountains, in the rocks and in the gullies, there is more gold and more silver than the world has ever yet heard of. The new Gulf republic must take in New Mexico, and

Arizona, and California, and it will become the treasure-house of all the time to come. We are poor now, but we shall be the richest people on earth. Only we must understand one thing at the outset. Gold is like freedom. Every pound of it that was ever won was somehow paid for in blood. I'm ready to give mine, right here, if I'm called for. Now I'm going in for a hammock. I'm clean used up."

It was past the middle of February, in the year 1836. The weather had been stormy, but was now better, bearing few traces of winter as it is in more northerly latitudes. It was a season of the year that could be expected to favor military movements, but the Mexican commander had been disappointed and seriously delayed during all the earlier part of his invasion. The rains and mud had been in the way of heavy provision-trains and artillery.

A little after sunrise on the morning after the arrival of the returning raiders, the sentry relieved at the Alamo gate-way reported the departure, an hour earlier, of Castro and his son.

"Gone on a scout," said Travis. "Hope they'll have good luck. We don't know half enough just now."

All that day was spent by the small garrison of the fort in what they called getting ready for a better state of things. They expected reinforcements and supplies, but Crockett and Bowie, rather than even Travis, insisted upon putting all they had in the best possible order. A strict account of rations was taken. Cannon were carefully cleaned, and most of them needed it. Every weapon, large or small, was brought out for inspection or repairs. Every ounce of powder was measured as if it were gold. At least a dozen men were kept at work moulding bullets, and for this purpose a number of leaden filigree ornaments were taken from the window casings of the old church.

"Best that can be did with 'em," remarked Crockett. "Church lead is as good as any other to kill Greasers with."

The supply of water was sure, for the Spanish builders had constructed aqueducts which brought an abundance, like springs within the walls.

The men were in high spirits over their work, and even Colonel Bowie lost some of the gloom which had been upon his face.

"Crockett," he remarked, however, "I hope

Houston 'll make good time. We shan't be ready for Santa Anna an hour too soon."

"Travis hardly believes he's comin'," replied Crockett. "He reckons the old monte-player will strike for the middle of the State and the coast towns."

"Not and leave the Alamo behind him," said Bowie. "We'll have the first fight right here, and it 'll be a hard one."

So they talked and worked, and the day passed and another night came and went. It was a little after the middle of the next day that a brace of mustangs were reined in upon the brow of a low hill looking southward.

"Ugh!" exclaimed one of them. "Red Wolf heap look. Santa Anna come!"

The younger rider was silent, but he was looking. For the first time in their lives they had seen an army. The southerly prairie was nearly level, traversed along its farther border by a winding stream of water. On this side of the stream, in long lines, in columns and in detachments, marched several regiments of infantry attended by batteries of light artillery. On their flanks and in the advance rode strong bodies of lancers. There were flags and pennons, and the serried bayonets wore a warlike look.   There were even bands of music.

"Heap Mexican!" exclaimed Red Wolf. "Tell Big Knife."

"Alamo men all die," replied Castro.

He did not move, however, during several minutes, for the bugles of the lancers and the shouted orders of the infantry commanders had called a halt.   Very shortly there were sufficient indications that the invading force had marched far enough for that day and that it was now going into camp.

It was by no means a perfectly organized army, and there was a sad lack of precision in its movements, but its dispositions for camping were tolerably well made.   Tents were put up for officers, but the rank and file were expected, evidently, to bivouac.   There would be little hardship in that, but if the Lipan scouts had been able to make a closer inspection, they might have noted that the entire array of over five thousand men wore a hard-travelled, worn-out appearance, as if they had been pushed and as if it were really about time that they should have a rest.

There were clumps of trees on the prairie. Wood could be cut and fires could be made, but before the first smoke began to rise Castro wheeled his horse.

"Ugh!" he said. "Ride now. Kill pony. Comanche no come."

He had been staring at point after point to discover if any of his old enemies were acting with the Mexicans. If they were, none of them could as yet be seen among the troops of Santa Anna.

He and his son disappeared over the rolls of the prairie, and, unless they should be intercepted, there would be news for the garrison of the Alamo.

Not in the centre of the Mexican camp, but on the bank of the river, a large and nearly new marquee tent had been put up as the first order for a halt was given. At a little distance a fire had been quickly kindled and cooking was already going on. In front of the tent stood a group of officers and they were chatting merrily.

"We will crush the Alamo like an eggshell," asserted one of them.

"It will surrender at discretion on our arrival," added another.

"Travis will never be so foolhardy as to resist an overwhelming force," remarked a third;

but he added to the dark-faced man in the middle of the group, " General, what are we to do after dinner ?   I'm tired of inspecting."

" So are the men," responded the general. " I think we shall have something better.   We can empty a coop."

He pointed as he spoke at a spot of ground fifty yards from the tent, at the right, where several ragged *peons* were at work with stakes and cord.   They were already constructing a cockpit, for the Mexican commander did not propose to let so small a matter as the conquest of Texas deprive him of his favorite amusement. Moreover, on the bank of the river, beyond the cockpit, were drawn up two large wagons, and each of these was almost over-piled with wicker coops, the occupants of which were from time to time crowing defiantly at each other.   If the army was to rest there while the Texans were getting ready to receive it, more than one of the coops might possibly be emptied by the proposed combats of the gallant poultry.

Meantime, the disposition of battalions, regiments, and batteries was left haphazard to subordinates who had no fowls to think of, and the general and his brilliant staff went in to dinner.

CHAPTER XVII.

THE FIRST SHOT.

FOUR days went by. All the space inside the walls of the fort had a clean and tidy look. The soldiers of the garrison went hither and thither with an air of being under more than usual drill, but their varied uniforms were about the same as ever. A light rain was falling and the skies overhead were heavy with clouds, as if a storm were coming.

A shout was heard outside the gate, and then its massive oaken portal swung wide open, while Colonel Travis stood by the six-pounder, his handsome face bright with expectation.

"Boys!" he shouted, "the supplies have come!"

Nearing the gate-way was a train of large wagons, and on either side and in the rear of them rode mounted riflemen.

"Reinforcements, too!" exclaimed Crockett, as he strode forward to the side of Travis.

Colonel Bowie was already out beyond the

242

wall, scrutinizing the approaching train and its guard.

"Not a quarter as many men as we needed," he remarked, in a low, foreboding tone. "I hope there are more coming."

On rolled the wagons, while cheer after cheer went up from the garrison, to be answered as heartily by the new arrivals.

"Keep right on," shouted Travis to the drivers. "Halt in front of the church."

The last pair of wheels was in the gate-way when galloping past them came a half-naked rider.

"Whoop!" he yelled. "Red Wolf want Big Knife. Castro horse dead. Santa Anna come!"

"All right!" called out Travis. "Come this way. Bowie, bring him in. Men, go on unloading. Tally all there is."

Down from his panting pony dropped the young Lipan, and his eager report required few questions to make it clear. Either his father had not been so well mounted or else he had been too heavy a weight for a long race. His horse had given out entirely a few miles from the fort, and Red Wolf had ridden on alone.

All the officers of the rangers had gathered to hear, and when the report was completed they looked at each other with serious faces.

"It's just about as we expected, after all," said Travis. "I'm glad there are no Comanches with them. If Castro is right, there are over five thousand of them. A thousand more or less won't make much difference. They're about four days' march from us, I should say, but the lancers could get here sooner. Most likely they will."

A rugged-looking ranger stood before him, touching a ragged hat-brim.

"Well, Sergeant Daly," said Travis, "how do you find the cargo?"

"Bully, far as it goes!" responded the sergeant. "I reckon it gives us rations for about two weeks. Pretty good lot of rifle powder. Not so much cannon powder and grape-shot as we'd ought to have. No solid shot to speak of, but there's some. Forty spare rifles, and I wish we had men for 'em. But these yer new men are all prime fellers, and we can foot up one hundred and forty good shots, all told."

"We ought to have at least three times as

many," said Travis. "Every man is worth his weight in gold just now."

"The trouble is," remarked Bowie, "Houston hasn't had time yet to use those Spanish dollars. He will, though. What we must do is to try and hold the fort till Austin's riflemen get here. Every day 'll count. Santa Anna is a slow marcher."

"You're mistaken thar," exclaimed Crockett. "If his Greasers could fight as well as they kin walk, we'd be gone up sure!"

The next duties related to the unloading of the wagons and to all the information that could be obtained from the new men. Even while Travis was talking with them, however, an hour or so later, a hand touched his arm, and he turned to look into the face of Castro.

"What is it, chief?" he asked.

"Close gate," said Castro. "Load big gun. Lancer! Bring pony in."

"They mean to make a dash for our corral, do they?" replied Travis, and orders for the care of the horses of the garrison went out at once.

It would not do to lose them all just now, and they, at least, would have abundant rations within the enclosure. One of the best of them was turned over to Castro in place of his used-up pony, and another as good was given to Red Wolf.

While this was going on, Bowie had been busy with the spare rifles that had just arrived, and now he made his appearance, carrying two weapons that were more ornamental than the rest, for both were silver mounted.

"Travis," he said, "this is for the chief, and this is the one I promised Red Wolf."

"They've earned 'em," exclaimed Crockett. "Give 'em a first-rate outfit. Hope they'll kill a grist of Greasers."

Colonel Travis himself presented the rifles, but his words were few. Castro took his own and examined it all over.

"Ugh!" he said. "Heap shoot. Travis kill Mexican with big gun. Red Wolf take rifle. Come!"

Red Wolf's eyes had been glittering with delight. Never before had he heard of an Indian boy of his age owning a really first-class rifle with all its accoutrements of wiping-stick, ramrod, powder-horn, and bullet-pouch. Those were the days of flintlocks, and the long-barrelled shooting-irons did not need any "cap-box" to go with them.

He was hardly expected to say much, but he made out to tell the colonel,—

"Red Wolf shoot a heap. Mexican lose hair. Wipe out Comanche."

As he finished speaking, however, Bowie himself laid a hand on his shoulder.

"Red Wolf go with his father now," he said. "Come back to Big Knife. Chief, let him come as soon as you can."

He had understood a sentence that Castro had uttered in his own tongue with its accompanying "sign."

"Chief send boy," replied Castro. "Go now. Travis fight a heap."

The two Lipans were upon the backs of their fresh mustangs the next minute, and they rode out of the gate as if some errand of importance hurried them.

"Reckon they think we've got our work cut out for us," said Crockett.

"They've seen the Mexican army," replied Bowie, "and they know just what's coming. So do we, but we mustn't say anything to dis-courage the men."

A watcher at a loop-hole saw Castro and Red Wolf wheel around the corner of the wall and gallop westward, but before he could report the direction they had taken the garrison was startled by the roar of a cannon from one of the southern embrasures. There had been a reason for the course taken by the Lipans.

"Who fired that gun?" shouted Travis, angrily. "Who fired without orders?"

"I did," came promptly back from Sergeant Daly. "I had the best kind of a bead on that crowd of lancers. It was only a four-pound shot, but it ploughed right into 'em."

"Not another charge is to be wasted," replied Travis. "We need every kernel. We were none too quick about the corral, though."

"Travis," said Bowie, quietly, "our time's about come. Houston must send us more men or we can't so much as man the walls."

It was a matter of course that a strong body of cavalry had been sent on in advance of the invading army. No doubt there had been an idea of striking the rebellious Texans at every possible point. The lancers, however, had not met with anything to strike at, and all they now could do, apparently, was to reconnoitre the fort. It was in a spirit of entirely empty bravado that they had approached so near or else they had forgotten that the Alamo had any artillery. They had at last halted, while their commander deliberately scanned the post and its surroundings through his field-glass.

Bang! went the four-pounder, and Daley's aim had been first-rate.

" *Caramba !*" roared the colonel. " My baggage mule! My equipments! Santa Maria! My cigarettes!"

Over went a fine mule, certainly, as the four pounds of iron arrived, but not because of anything that prevented him from getting up at once and braying. Upon his patient back, rising above the panniers that adorned his flanks, had been a load more large than heavy. It was this hump of varied luxury and usefulness into which the sergeant's wasteful shot had ploughed.

Mexico had not lost even so much as a mule, but the ground was strewn with cigarettes and other merchandise, and the lancer force had been warned that they were in front of a battery.

"Fellow-citizens!" shouted the angry officer. "Heroes of Mexico! Yonder is the Alamo! In a few days we will ride into it and teach the Gringo rebels a lesson they will remember. Forward, right wheel! Gallop!"

Gallop they did, but Travis's order to save ammunition had already put them entirely out of danger.

Miles away to the westward rode Castro and his son, but the chief had now gone far enough for the purpose which had taken him away from the fort. He drew his rein and Red Wolf imitated him.

"Ugh!" said Castro, holding out a hand. "Rifle!"

The splendid present was handed over, but other commands followed, and the young warrior was stripped of his bow and arrows, his lance and his pistols. His only remaining weapon was the knife in his belt. There was not a shadow of disobedience, not even of dissatisfaction, upon his face, but he was evidently waiting for an explanation.

"Red Wolf no lose rifle," said Castro, at last. "Great chief take it to lodge. Hide it with tribe."

" Ugh ?" said Red Wolf, but he knew there was something more to come.

" No bad medicine," said Castro, holding out his hand again.

The three gold bars allotted to Red Wolf were tightly secured to his saddle. They were now untied and handed over. The chief dropped from his pony and walked to the nearest oak, one of three by which they had halted. He took out his knife, dug a pretty deep hole, and dropped the precious but dangerous prizes into it.

Red Wolf had followed him in silence, and now, when the earth and sods were replaced, Castro stood erect and pointed at the spot under which lay the gold.

" All Texan lose hair," he said. " Red Wolf hide bad medicine. Find some day ! Die then. Montezuma wicked manitou."

" Ugh !" exclaimed Red Wolf.

Nevertheless, a deep " sign" was cut upon the oak-tree before they remounted. Then the chief went on to explain to his son the further duties required of him.

It did not take a great many words, but the meaning of it all was simple.

The Mexicans and the Lipans were now nominally at peace. Any Lipan was fairly safe
among them, unless he should seem to be on a
war-path against them. At the same time,
Mexican cavalry would surely disarm a mere
boy,—that is, they would steal his rifle, even
if they then should let him go unharmed.

So far, so good, but Castro raised his arm
and pointed eastward.

"Boy hear!" he said. "Travis send Texan
to friend? Mexican catch ranger. Shoot
him. No catch Red Wolf. Go! Ride hard!
Tell great Texan chief Santa Anna here! Say
he camp around Alamo. Say Travis want
more Texan. Ugh! Go!"

It was an errand of importance, therefore.
It was worthy of a warrior. It was a message
of life and death, but it called for cunning,
caution, hard riding, rather than for sharp-
shooting. A few further instructions as to
where to go and whom to find were all that
was needed, and away went the ready messenger.

Castro himself rode away, laden with the
precious shooting-irons. He too had need for
caution and for cunning if he was ever to re-

join his tribe, but Red Wolf, riding northward now, was saying to himself,—

"Ugh! Heap young brave. Bring Texan to Big Knife. Heap fight Mexican."

He may have been perfectly aware that Colonel Travis was the white chief who was in actual command of the rangers and the fort. To his mind, however, the Texan armies, if not the republic itself, were best represented by the stalwart hand-to-hand fighter who had given him the knife which he now so carefully concealed under his buckskins. Having done so, he transferred his old, half-despised butcher-knife from his leggings to his belt, and remarked concerning it, " Mexican take? Ugh! No lose heap knife. Take Mexican hair."

There was a menacing look in his face, and he rode on with the air of an adventurer who was quite ready for mischief, if a chance for any should be given him.

The region of country he was to go through was supposed to be peaceable, as yet. It contained only scattered ranches and small settlements, but it might speedily contain almost anything else, for perils of all sorts were pouring in upon the Texas border.

Matters at the fort were quiet, but the rangers in their quarters, even while running bullets, and the officers in their hammocks, not one of them asleep, seemed to have constituted themselves a kind of general council of war. At least they were discussing every feature of the situation, and were talking themselves more and more into a state of mind that bordered closely upon contempt for Santa Anna and his five thousand men.

The most undemonstrative man among them all was Colonel Bowie. He had slung his hammock near one of the embrasures, with a cannon at his side, and, like the cannon, he was continually peering out. Even after it grew darker and only moonlight remained to show him anything, he every now and then seemed to take an inquiring look at the surrounding country.

"I can see that cave," he muttered to himself, "as clear as if I were in it. What if the fate of a young nation should depend upon our getting into that hole again? If those old rascals knew we·were coming, they'd pitch it all down the chasm. I'd like to know, just for curiosity, what fellows and how many of them have been butchered before that altar. In the old times they used up whole tribes and regiments of captives that way. Then I'd like to know where all that bullion came from. I don't believe they mined for it. They didn't know how. They got it out of river-beds, I reckon, just as they do in Asia and Africa."

He had hit the mark, for there was no other way imaginable. But where were the river-beds, and how much more gold-dust and nuggets might there be remaining in them?

He could dream and speculate there in his hammock, but that was all he could do. His young republic was indeed to come and go. Mexico was to lose Texas and her other northern provinces. The pioneers among whom he was so daring a leader were to accomplish even more than they were planning. Beyond all his dreams, however, would be the solution of his gold problem. Only a few years later the slopes and gulches of the California mountains were to swarm with hardy miners, and the treasures of the Montezumas were to sink into insignificance in comparison with the wealth to be taken out, not by the Aztecs or the Spaniards, but by the " Gringos."

Would anybody then be found to take note of the fact that Bowie and his comrades were the advance-guard, the skirmish-line, almost the "forlorn hope" of the armies of Taylor and Scott? The United States, the world at large, and even Mexico, owe their memories something of recognition, and they were not even much "ahead of their time."

"Crockett," said Travis, just before they went to sleep, "Bowie can't get that cave out of his head."

"It's t'other way," replied Crockett. "He can't get his head out of the cave, and I'll be glad, you bet, when we all get our heads out of the cave this push of Santa Anna is putting us into."

CHAPTER XVIII.

FEBRUARY 24, 1836, and a splendid winter morning for a parade.

Altogether unmolested as they came, the Mexican army marched into position around the Alamo fort. Not a shot was fired at them. Not a man of the garrison was in sight. There was a sullen air about the whole concern. Upon the church wall, indeed, Colonel Travis with a field-glass studied and estimated the assailants he was to contend with.

"No heavy guns, Davy," he said to Crockett, standing near him. "Castro was right about everything else. We shall get a message from Santa Anna pretty soon. Hullo! There he comes now. Let's go down."

"You've only jest one thing to do," replied Crockett, dryly, at the head of the stairs they were to go down by.

"What's that?" said Travis, getting ready for a joke. "Out with it."

"Well" chuckled the bear hunter, one stair down, "you know what he's goin' to ask for. Just you demand the immediate, onconditional surrender of Santa Anna and all his chickens."

"Crockett!" exclaimed Travis, "I can tell you one thing. I know him. If we should surrender, no matter what conditions he might give, the old murderer would have every man of us shot before sunset."

"Not a doubt of it," said Crockett; "and between you and me and the gate-post, I'd ruther do a small chance of hard fighting first. That's about the way the men feel, too."

That was the kind of reputation the Mexican general had won for himself, and he was shortly to add to it by his conduct of his campaign in Texas.

By the time the two friends came out through the church door-way, the officer of the guard at the gate was loudly responding to a sonorous bugle summons. A mounted officer, attended by the bugler only, had halted outside.

"A cartel from His Excellency General de Santa Anna!" he shouted, in response to the hail of the sergeant. "I am accredited to Señor Travis."

In rode the very airy captain of lancers.

"Colonel Travis, you mean!" shouted back the sergeant, angrily; but the clear, ringing tones of Bowie called out,—

"Let him in, Daly. Never mind his nonsense."

Open swung the gate, and in rode the very airy captain of lancers who had been sent to demand the surrender of the fort, but who had insolently neglected to acknowledge the military rank of its commander.

That was the sum and substance of the letter he shortly delivered to Travis, after dismounting and exchanging formal compliments. Added to it, however, was the grim assurance that, in case of resistance, the fort would be stormed at once and no quarter whatever would be shown to the garrison.

"Good!" said Travis, smilingly. "No use in my writing. Go back to the general and tell him to come on. We are ready."

"Is that all?" exclaimed the astonished captain. "Are you mad? Do you really intend to resist us?"

"Travis," whispered Crockett, "tell him to say that if they'll march right hum and agree to stay thar, we won't hurt a soul of 'em."

The captain heard him, and his astonishment showed itself more plainly, but the reply of Travis was strictly formal.

"That is all," he said. "He knows me. Tell him I am in command here. We shall hold the Alamo!"

Low bowed the captain, turning to his horse, and in a moment more he was spurring beyond the gate, and it closed clangingly behind him. There was really nothing more for the bugler to do, but he blew his horn furiously before he galloped away.

"It'll take something better'n bugle music to get the Greasers over those walls," remarked Crockett; but the long eighteen-pounder was now at one of the southerly embrasures, and, at a signal from Travis, a thunder of defiance rang out.

"That's the last blank cartridge we'll fire," said Travis. "Now let's see what they'll do next. The fools can't really mean to try to storm the works? I almost wish they would."

"If he'd said he'd do it to-day, he'll put it off till to-morrow," replied Crockett, sarcastically. "He never kept his word since he was born,—except about throat-cutting."

No other voice responded. Quiet, resolute, cheerful, the picked men who constituted that heroic garrison were at their stations, and not a quiver of fear showed itself among them. As for the enemy, Crockett had not been far out of the way. Postponement was second nature to Santa Anna. Besides, he was really possessed of considerable military education and ability. He could see that, as the rangers said among themselves, "he had a pretty hard nut to crack." He would therefore think about it during the rest of that day. All he was ready to do at once was to send his heaviest battery into position and order it to blaze away. It was composed of very handsomely polished brass nine-pounder guns. It swept into its place with a flourish of brass music from the bands and a sounding of many drums.

"There will be a breach in the wall before sunset," declared the general, confidently. "We can charge in to-morrow."

Loudly roared the guns, and they were good ones, but praise did not await the artillerymen. One shot struck the wall of the church. Another went over the fort. The remainder fell short and ploughed deep furrows in the sandy soil.

"Santa Maria!" exclaimed the colonel of artillery. "We must do better next time."

The six guns of the battery were reloaded. Every piece was aimed with care, and off they went again.

"How is it, Crockett?" shouted Travis to his friend, for the eccentric satirist was sitting on the wall, his legs dangling outside, and he was leaning forward.

"Two on 'em hit the wall, replied Crockett. "Dented it some. Tell Daly to come around and see the holes."

"Bowie," said Travis, "you and Daly. Don't let another man out. His next battery is nearly ready to open fire."

It was quite ready, but it was composed of lighter pieces. A minute or so later, Bowie and the sergeant were out in front talking to Crockett on the wall.

"They've damaged it a little," said Daly. "I don't like the looks of it."

"Could they punch a hole through," asked Davy, "if they hammered long enough?"

"Reckon they could," remarked Bowie. "I think that's our worst danger. But I want to hear from those other guns."

Two batteries sounded this time, and the three Texans stood still and watched with deep interest the effect of the shots. It did not seem to occur to either of them that a cannon-ball might possibly hurt a man.

"Right over my head," said Crockett, quietly. "Hit the roof of the convent."

"Hurrah!" shouted Daly. "Them nine-pound balls punch, but the sixes don't make a mark worth a cent. They can jest thunder away."

"Come on," said Bowie. "Let's go in. If they had heavier guns there'd be a breach in that wall pretty soon. Anything smaller'n sixes would be like pelting us with apples."

Santa Anna did not seem to be of that opinion. Or else he may have calculated that sharp cannonading would dishearten the garrison. His own troops evidently enjoyed it, but there was a severe shock awaiting the distinguished Mexican. Again and again his heaviest battery had spoken thunderously, and he felt sure that it must have accomplished something, but now before him stood General Castrillon, in command of all the artillery of the invading army. His face was red, his mous-

taches seemed to curl with wrath, and his first
utterances were half choked with furious execrations upon the army commissary at Monterey.

"What is the matter, general?" sternly demanded the commander-in-chief.

"No more nine-pound shot!" roared General Castrillon. "The miscreant has loaded
the other wagon with twelve-pound balls!
They are useless!"

"*Caramba!*" almost screamed his chief. "I
will have him shot! Let the cannonading
cease. The fort must be taken by escalade.
Have the ladders ready by nine o'clock to-
morrow morning."

The fort was safer, but an admirable example had been given of the inefficiency, in-
dolence, and general worthlessness of the Mexican officials. Not even the probability of being
shot for their blunders could induce them to
discharge their duties thoroughly.

"That battery's tired out," remarked Crockett, as the pause in the firing grew longer.
"Reckon they're holdin' on while they can take
a game of seven-up. They haven't hurt us any."

"Yes, they have," said Travis, quietly.
"Don't you see? Or haven't you been up

the church again? They're swinging their camps around to make a blockade."

"They can't choke us off that way," responded Crockett. "Thar ain't enough of 'em. If they'll string out in as long a line as would go' round, it 'll be thin all the way. I'd go a-gunning anywhar along that line."

"That isn't the point," said Travis. "He's arranging to cut off reinforcements. He knows how many men we have, you can bet on that. He doesn't mean to let any more in."

"The kind of men that are coming," growled Crockett, "are likely to find a way in or make one. But it's about time they were here."

"I'm going to send a despatch to Houston," said Travis. "Carson has volunteered to take it."

"Well," returned Crockett, "most likely he'll know without our tellin', but what if Carson doesn't get through?"

"We must take our chances," said Travis. "One man's all we can spare. "I'm almost afraid Houston can't send any more to us just now."

"Every man in Texas owns a rifle!" exclaimed Crockett, with energy. "Not a livin' soul ought to stay at home."

"Pay and rations," said Travis, calmly. "I'm afraid Bowie's dollars didn't come in time. It isn't any fault of his, but all the gold in Mexico wouldn't save the Alamo."

Bowie was listening, but he turned away without speaking, for he was questioning himself. Was it any fault of his? Had it been his duty to return at once with the cash found in the *adobe* ruin instead of pushing on with Tetzcatl? It was a serious question, but at last he put it away.

"Come what may," he told himself, "I could not have done otherwise. I had no choice. I was driven. I was in one of those places where a man cannot decide for himself. The Comanches did it."

The movements of the several assignments of the Mexican army went on deliberately all through the day. The circle that was made was pretty long, however, and there were gaps between the camps which would require careful patrolling to make complete what Crockett described as "the corral of the Gringos."

"Anything like a provision-train, for instance," remarked Bowie, "couldn't get in without a battle. There isn't any American force yet gathered in Texas that could undertake to whip an army of five thousand men."

Night came at last, and with it came a moon instead of the darkness which Travis had been wishing for. It was not a good night for a secret messenger, and the mounted patrols of the enemy were going to and fro almost up to the walls of the fort.

"Their infantry outlooks are well out in advance of their lines," remarked Travis, standing in the gate-way. "I doubt if it's possible for Carson to get through."

"If I thought he couldn't I'd go myself," exclaimed Bowie. "I wish he were an Indian!"

"That's jest what I am," came from the brave ranger who had volunteered. "I've crept through a band of Chickasaws. My skelp isn't wuth as much as Bowie's is, anyhow. It's no use in talkin'. I'm off."

"You bet he is," quietly remarked a voice behind them, "and I'm goin' with him the first stretch."

There stood Davy Crockett, rifle in hand.

"I'd feel better if you would," said Bowie. "You're an older hand than he is. See him as far as their lines and take note of everything, —and come back."

" Come back ?" chuckled Davy.   " Of course I will.   I'll have some fun, too.   Get along, Carson.   I'm goin' to take keer of ye.   You're young."

Off they went, and Travis laughed aloud as they disappeared.

" You wait now," he said.   " Davy's goin' to stir up the Greasers somehow before he gets done with 'em, but I can't guess what the sell is."

It would have been only a very sombre life-and-death affair to men of another kind, but these were hardly excited to any unusual feeling.   They were in the daily habit of looking death in the face, and they could laugh at him. Nevertheless, during many minutes that followed, they and a changing group of rangers waited in the gate-way, listening silently to every sound that came to them from the hostile camps.   A troop of horse went trampling by within a hundred yards of them and they heard the words of command.   More minutes passed and the stillness seemed to increase.

" We'd have heard something if the Greasers

had sighted 'em," whispered one of the men. "They're not took yet——"

"Hear that gun!" shouted Travis, the next instant. "That means something!"

Another cannon sounded, and another, and then they heard the rapid reports of musketry from a score of points all along the lines.

"Bad luck!" groaned a ranger.

"They've got 'em!" said another.

"It's good-by, Davy Crockett, I'm afraid," said Bowie, in a voice that was deep with emotion. "We ought not to have let him go."

The expressions of regret for him and Carson were many and sincere, all around, but the cunning old bear hunter had been doing a remarkable piece of what passed with him for fun.

Only about ten minutes before the first alarm gun sounded a pair of shadows had been gliding along on the ground, midway between the two camps that were nearest to the fort gate.

"So far, so good," whispered one of them. "What's best to do next?"

"Straight into the corral," was the reply. "I allers feel at hum among hosses. They're kind o' friendly. Besides, you've got to hev one to travel on."

A very large number of them, of all sorts, had been picketed there, a short distance in the rear of the camps. They were guarded, of course, but they were entirely out of the supposable reach of Gringo thieves from the fort, and the guards were taking things easily. So were the quadrupeds, and not one of them was at all disturbed in his mind when two men who might belong to the same army slipped silently in among them.

"No Greaser kin see through a hoss," remarked one of the adventurers, "but I'll tell you what, my boy, your tightest squeeze is goin' to be in gettin' out on the further side. They're guardin' thar rear more'n they are toward the fort. They're on the watch for anything Sam Houston may let loose on 'em."

That was in strict accordance with the military prudences of the situation, but for that very reason all the guards on duty were looking out instead of looking in. No patrol, for instance, beyond the camps, whether mounted or on foot, could at once imagine anything suspicious concerning a dim shape slowly tramping out from the horse corral. Only one did come, and he walked along leading with him a saddled and bridled mustang.

" Here comes the guard !" he suddenly exclaimed, aloud. " Now's my time. I'll signal to Davy."

He sprang upon the back of the mustang, turned and blew a short, sharp whistle, and galloped away. Hundreds of men may have heard the whistle, but only one understood it. Not a solitary Mexican at once followed the vanishing horseman, and he quickly was beyond successful following.

Hoarse shouts had gone after him, truly. Orders to halt, with Spanish inquiries and execrations, had sounded from all directions. It was understood that something or other had happened, and there were officers who at once began to investigate the matter.

The proper direction of their first efforts was plainly indicated by an extraordinary disturbance in the corral. Quite a large number of the horses were now loose and they were running around excitedly. It did not arise to the dignity of a stampede, but the guards who first rushed in came near being trampled down. These were joined at once by the too zealous sentries of a battery which had been stationed at the right of the corral, so that its guns were for the moment left to take care of themselves.

"Don't I wish I had some spikes?" inquired a very low, hoarse chuckle that was crawling along at the side of one of the guns. "If I had I'd spile every touch-hole of this 'ere battery. Hullo! Thar they are. I reckon I kin shew 'em a new p'int in the right way of handlin' artillery. That is, if ary one of these long fours is primed."

After that there came a clicking of flint and steel, and then a soft glow of fire close to the ground.

Louder grew the tumult in the corral, angrier and more numerously arose the shouts and commands of the officers.

"Jim Carson's got clean away from 'em, I reckon," was spoken more loudly, "but that lot of Greasers have marched to about the right spot. Wonder what this thing is shotted with. Here she goes!"

A hand went up to the breech of the gun and then the first booming alarm went out.

"Reckon 'twas a round shot," he said. "It fetched 'em. One more."

A second gun spoke out, and then a third, in quick succession, but to Mexican ears it seemed the correct thing for any of their own guns to do in case of a sudden alarm at night. It would show the garrison that its besiegers were awake.

Nevertheless, the iron missiles had been sent with deadly effect among the luckless detachment of infantry, and every man of it who was left unhurt fired off his musket at the space in front of him and the possible Gringos it might contain. Sentry after sentry, all along, in camp after camp, followed that example, front and rear. The very game-cocks in their coops crowed vigorously, and the general himself came out of his tent to see what was the matter with them and with his army.

The artillerymen who now came hurrying back to their guns found no one with them,— nothing but an entirely unexplainable mystery. There were now no soldiers in front of the battery, however. The coast was clear, and across the moonlit area from which he had driven his enemies Davy Crockett strode on to the Alamo.

"Who goes there?" greeted him from the sentry at the gate.

"I ain't a-goin' jest now; I'm comin'," shouted back the very grim old joker, with a fierce laugh. "Travis, I reckon Jim Carson's all right. We took him a good mount from thar own corral. But I fired them alarm guns myself. Wait till I git in and I'll tell jest how I did it, but I reckon the Greasers 'll think we've made a *sortee*."

Three cheers were given him, and these too were heard by the Mexicans to increase their perplexity. Something very like a *sortie* had really been made, and the entire Mexican army was getting under arms. One regiment marched a mile before it could be ordered back, but Santa Anna himself had preserved his military composure.

"*Caramba!*" he exclaimed, in reply to one of his officers. "Houston? No! He has no force that he can send. We have nothing to deal with but the desperadoes inside of yonder walls, and we shall slaughter them to-morrow."

CHAPTER XIX.

A WAY outside of the fort wall at sunrise stood Davy Crockett, all alone. He had been noting with evident interest the marks made upon the masonry by the cannon-balls fired the day before.

"All right," he said. "It amuses them and it doesn't hurt us. I'm only fifty, and my ha'r will be turnin' gray before they git in this way."

It was a satisfactory conclusion, and he turned to scan the Mexican lines.

"Jim Carson got away from them," he said. "Of course he did, but we can't wait for Sam Houston. We've got to depend on ourselves. Well, now! If this isn't curious! Whoever heard of Greasers gittin' up early? I didn't, but they're a-movin'. Reckon we're goin' to have some fun right away."

That was the opinion of Travis and two ranger officers up in the church tower.

The camps of the Mexican infantry were

pouring forth their bayonets, and everywhere the cavalrymen stood beside their horses, ready to mount at the word of command. What was to be done with horsemen in an attack upon stone walls did not appear, but the telescope revealed much more ominous preparations. Already out in front of the southerly camps were parties of men who were provided with ladders. If the artillery as yet had made no breaches, the walls could be climbed over. The cannon were to have their share in the day's work nevertheless, and at a given signal every battery began to speak. A storm of iron pellets hurtled against the defences or flew over them.

That part of the fortress which was mainly composed of the church and of the convent did not promise well for a climbing adventure. The assaulting force was therefore massed for a rush against the lower walls around the plaza. These were pierced for musketry as well as for cannon. Every shot-hole had now its marksman, with two more standing behind him ready, each to take his place in turn while the others reloaded.

" Let 'em come close up," was the order of

Colonel Travis. "Hit every man just below his belt."

"And ef you do," added Crockett, "that thar Greaser 'll sit right down."

Low voices passed from man to man, and the substance of the utterances was,—

"Hit, boys! Every shot is for life."

An iron calmness grew harder in all their faces as the fire of the batteries ceased and the Mexican masses began to move steadily forward to the sound of their drums. They came on as confidently as if the fort were already their own, for their officers were freely declaring the expectation that at the last moment the Gringos would give up so hopeless a defence and surrender.

That is, the nerves of the rangers or of their commander, proof against the thunders of the artillery, were to fail at the prospect of being crushed by overwhelming numbers. Perhaps the very silence that reigned around the fort did something to increase the delusion, and the foremost ranks advanced to within short rifle range.

"Ain't I glad the grape-shot and canister got here in time!" growled Sergeant Daly, squinting along his gun.

"Ready!" shouted Travis at that moment from the middle of the plaza. "All ready! Let 'em have it! Fire!"

Every cannon of the fort which bore upon the enemy went off as if one hand had fired them all. A storm of lead and iron swept through the advancing columns. Then as the smoke-clouds cleared away a little the cracking of the rifles began, and the astonished Mexicans dropped rapidly, only too many of them smitten "just below the belt" or a few inches above it.

The attempt to overawe the garrison by a sudden attack in force had signally failed. It had become little better than a disastrous reconnoitring party. Nothing had been really ready for so serious an undertaking as the storming of the Alamo. The Mexican troops were marched back to their camps, while their officers made up very disagreeable lists of killed and wounded.

The cannon of the fort had been very well handled and the accuracy of the rifle practice had been remarkable. At the same time, not a man of the garrison had received so much as a scratch. They could hardly believe that the battle was over.

"Jim Bowie," shouted Crockett, as he saw his friend coolly at work with a rifle-wiper, "none o' that jest now. Don't stop to clean your gun. Blaze away with it dirty and wipe it out by and by, after this butcher business is over. It hasn't been exactly a fight, not yit, but it's p'isonous fun for Santy Anny."

The Mexican general indeed was wild with rage and disappointment over the failure of his first ill-advised demonstration. For the first time in his varied military experience he had witnessed the effects of sharp-shooting.

He was not singular by any means. At that date the best infantry of Europe were still armed with smooth-bore muskets and depended mainly upon volley-firing when in action. The crack regiments of England, truly, had received a terrible lesson at New Orleans from the American riflemen under General Jackson, but neither the British nor any other military power had seemed willing to profit largely by it.

All military operations were over for the day. The batteries rested, and the commander-in-chief of the beaten army had not even the heart for his evening game of monte.

"Men!" said Colonel Travis to his gallant

garrison, drawn up for a kind of triumphant review in the plaza, " I don't mean to say much, but this is the kind of work that is going to save Texas."

" You bet it is, and thar's got to be heaps of it done," came in a low-voiced snarl from Crockett. " What they need is killing."

" The enemy have received a sharp lesson," continued Travis, " but they won't give it up right away. They can't afford to retreat after only one battle. Santa Anna would be kicked out of power if he should fail to take the Alamo. So if we can beat him completely we shall be setting both Texas and Mexico free from the old gambler's tyranny."

A loud cheer responded, and on the heels of the last " hurrah" Crockett remarked,—

" And we'll save our own throats, too, if that's any object. Mine was feelin' a little kind o' sore this mornin', but it's all right jest now."

The men went to their quarters and stations in very full accord with the feelings of the old bear hunter.

" Bowie," said Travis, as soon as they were alone together, " it's almost better than I hoped for. What do you think ?"

"There will be two or three days of cannonading," said Bowie. "Then there will be another attack. I reckon we can beat them off again. We haven't provisions for a long siege. They could starve us out."

"If they give Houston time enough," replied Travis, "he'll be operating on the outside of 'em somehow. They can't wait for too long a siege."

"We are not to die of starvation," said Bowie. "If it comes to that, we can walk out and die killing Mexicans. I will for one."

They were not at all deceived as to the desperate nature of their position. As for their patriotic commander-in-chief, he was struggling with a sea of troubles. Most of the money found in the old *adobe* had gone to New Orleans for arms and ammunition, but it might be weeks before there would be any important returns. He was using the remainder of the cash at home trying to get his hastily gathered volunteers into the shape of an army. He and Austin had several bodies of men at points distant from each other, but not one of them could be marched for the relief of the Alamo, nor would all of them together have been a third in number of the force under Santa Anna. Some of their commanders, to make the matter worse, seemed hardly to consider themselves under anybody's orders, so new and so unsettled was the authority of the Texan government.

It was toward the close of the day of that first attempt to storm the fort that a party of thirty-two mounted riflemen were somewhat leisurely pursuing their way along a road the western end of which was known to reach the town of San Antonio de Bexar. At their head rode a short, squarely built man, whose hat was pulled forward over his eyes. He was leaning a little, as if he were bent down by some weight or other.

"They are all there," he muttered. "The best men in Texas. They'll never give up. They'll die right whar they stand. Ye-es, sir! I'm goin'! I am! If it's only to go in and die alongside of Jim Bowie, and Travis, and old Davy!"

A shout rang out behind him, and it was instantly answered by an Indian war-whoop in front.

"Halt!" he promptly commanded as he raised his head, but he at once added, "Only one redskin. Who cares? What's up?"

The one redskin was trying in vain to urge an exhausted pony to a gallop.

" I'll ride forward and meet him," exclaimed the officer. "He's got something. I know Indians. Hold on, boys."

In a moment more he was listening to an eager voice that told him great news.

" Red Wolf," he said. " Heap Lipan. Son of Castro. Friend of Big Knife."

" But what are you here for?" interrupted the white leader. " I'm Colonel Smith."

" Travis heap want more Texan!" said Red Wolf. "Santa Anna come! All Mexican at fort. Heap big gun. More Texan come or all ranger lose hair. Castro great chief! Tell young brave ride heap! Bring many rifle! Ugh!"

" God bless you!" exclaimed Smith. " Bully for Castro! I know him."

Then he turned to his men and shouted,—

" Boys! It's all right! He's from the fort. Santa Anna's whole army is marching upon the Alamo. It's thar now!"

" We ought to ha' come quicker," was the first response that came from any of the men.

Smith could speak Spanish, however, and

Red Wolf was more at home in that tongue than in English. He now gave the colonel a full account of the scout he and his father had made ; of the arrival of the supply-train ; of the condition of things at the fort ; and of the estimated strength of the Mexican army. All that he said was at once communicated to the men, but it did not seem to dismay them. On the contrary, not one of them faltered when at last their commander addressed them with,—

"Men! Now you know just how it is, how many of you are ready to push right on with me to the Alamo?"

"Git right along," came cheerily back from one of the riflemen. "Thar ain't any white feathers a-flyin' in this crowd. We're all with ye. Hurrah for Texas!"

"Forward, march!" shouted the colonel. "Every mile is worth blood. Boy, let 'em give you another mount. That thar mustang o' your'n is played out."

There was no more travel in him, at all events, and he was quickly turned loose to shift for himself, while all that had been on him was going westward upon a comparatively fresh and lively pony.

"It 'll be about two days' riding," remarked Smith, "at the rate we'll have to go. When we get thar, we'll have to take our chances for findin' our way into the fort."

"We'll get in," they all agreed, but just how they expected to do it did not appear. On they rode, and their camp that night had the appearance of a picnic rather than of the bivouac of a handful of adventurers who were on their way to cut a path for themselves through a hostile army to almost certain death.

The Mexican general held a council of war that evening, and its session lasted late into the night, for there were ample refreshments upon the table in his marquee.

It was not a cheerful council, for the reports of the army surgeons were rendered, and they were unpleasant reading. So appeared to be several despatches which had but just arrived.

"General," exclaimed General Cos, when his commander had announced their contents, "the sinking of that barge in the Nueces is a greater disaster to us than is to-day's repulse. With those two heavy guns we could have made a breach in the wall in an hour."

"We must make one somehow," replied

Santa Anna, "since you all disapprove of a night assault. Castrillon, mass your batteries to-morrow and play all your shot upon one point. Make every shot tell. It's only a matter of time."

"So!" replied the artillery officer. "The breach can be made. And all the while the garrison will be eating up its supplies."

"So will we," laughed General Cos, "but we've a big drove of cattle coming. We can live on beef and water till we have crushed this den of Gringo tigers."

The tigers themselves in their fort-den were resting quietly, all but one, for the commander of the Alamo was pacing up and down slowly, thoughtfully, in the plaza. No doubt it behooved him to be wakeful, but once, when he paused in his promenade, he said, half aloud,—

"I hope Jim Carson got through. Crockett feels pretty sure that he did. Then my wife will get my last letter. I want her to know that I did my duty and died like a man. I had hoped to live in Texas and see it grow up to be something, but it's no use talking of that now. Our time has come. Not a man of us will ever get out of this place alive. And all

because Sam Houston can't raise cash enough
to feed his men on a march."

He laughed satirically, and the sentry at the
gate and the watchers at the loop-holes heard
him. It did them good to know that he was
so merry.

The night waned toward the dawn. Just in
the gray mist of the dark hour the riflemen
under Colonel Smith had risen and they were
busy around their camp-fires. They had no
idea of any enemy being near them, but suddenly they were startled by a loud "whoop!"

"That redskin!" shouted Smith, snatching
his rifle and dashing out of the camp. "Come
on, boys! Something's up!"

They were following fast, but he was well
ahead, and he came out into the road in time to
hear a shrill voice beyond him in the mist de-
manding,—

"Jim heap halt! Ugh! Red Wolf! Heap
Texan!"

"You young sarpent, are you here?" came
back from a man on horseback. "Do you
mean to say that some of our men are nigh
around?"

"Who goes thar?" shouted Smith.

"Carson, from the Alamo," responded the messenger. "Who are you?"

"Friend of Big Knife," suggested Red Wolf to the colonel. "Ranger."

"All right!" shouted back Smith. "Dismount and come in. We're on our way to jine the garrison. How are things?"

"Well," replied Carson, as he came to the ground, "when I came away Santa Anna had just fairly got into position. I had to snake it through his lines to carry despatches to Houston. Jest you look here, though. Don't you believe I left without orders. Somebody had to come. I'm coming right back to the fort soon as I've done my arr'nd."

"Bully for you!" shouted a rifleman. "That's what we're here for. Come along now and git yer rations."

"I might ha' gone by ye if it hadn't been for Red Wolf," said Carson, as they went along. "Bowie says he's the brightest chap of his age that he ever knew. He can't say that he ever saw him asleep. He can guide ye into the fort when you git thar."

"We'll git in," replied Smith. "I reckon Travis 'll be glad we met you. Every rifle's going to count in such a fight as this promises to be."

"You bet!" said Jim. "I felt bad about coming away, but I gave up my chance there to please Travis. You'll see me inside the walls before many days. You will!"

19

THE siege of the Alamo had lasted during eight long, terrible days. There had been a great deal of severe skirmishing, in which the Mexicans had suffered losses every time they drew too near the walls. The blockade, however, had become so close and vigilant that it was no longer possible for any bearer of despatches to get out or in. Out of several that had been sent, it was understood that two only had escaped capture and immediate execution. From those who had reached him General Houston was informed as to the condition of affairs at the fort. The deepest sympathy was felt for the beleaguered patriots and preparations for their relief were going on. Precious cargoes of army supplies had arrived from New Orleans in spite of Mexican war-vessels cruising in the Gulf. Troops were getting ready. One train of wagons accompanied by a force of riflemen was already a number

290

of miles upon its way, with a vague idea that it might somehow evade the army of Santa Anna. Men assured one another that if the garrison could only hold out a few days longer all would be well.

Colonel Travis and his men had held their own remarkably. They even seemed but little fatigued by their long watching, their readiness to be called to the shot-holes at any hour of day or night. They were exceedingly tough and hardy men. They would have been in good spirits if it had not been for two things. One of these sombre considerations was the condition of about ten yards of the southerly wall of the plaza. This was crumbling under the continual pelting of Castrillon's guns. Most of it was nearly level with the ground, and the gap had been feebly filled with such pieces of timber and other materials as could be had. Loose earth had been heaped upon them, but the slight barrier so constructed was at the mercy of cannon-balls. The other point was even more important.

"Colonel Travis," reported Sergeant Daly that morning, "thar's only half a dozen rounds for the cannon. The last ounce of pow-

der and the last bullet have been sarved out to
the men. Thar isn't enough for an hour's
shootin' if the next fight turns out a hot
one."

"Oh, God! If Houston knew!" groaned
the commander. "Why doesn't help come?
Daly, don't say a word to the men. It's possible that the Greasers may not make another
attack——"

"We've killed a heap of 'em," replied the
brave artilleryman. "But what on 'arth are
guns good for without ammunition?"

"We won't surrender, if we've nothing left
to fight with but our knives!"

"Colonel!" exclaimed Daly. "The men
wanted me to ask you that question. They
know just the fix we're in. You won't surrender?"

"I won't!" said Travis, firmly.

"Thank God!" almost shouted Daly. "We
want to die like men, with arms in our hands.
We don't want to be led out and butchered."

"The boys needn't be afraid that I'll go
back on 'em," replied the colonel. "I won't
rob them of their last rights. If we've got to
die, we'll go down fighting."

"That's all I wanted to know," said Daly, and away he strode to tell his comrades that they were in no danger of being betrayed unarmed into the hands of Santa Anna.

Hardly had he gone before there came a hail and a response at the great gate, and two men stood before it. One of them wore the uniform of the Mexican army and the other almost no uniform at all.

"Jim Carson! Castro!" had been loudly announced by the sentry.

"Let 'em in, quick!" shouted Travis. "You don't know who's behind 'em."

"Ugh!" exclaimed the chief as he stepped inside. "Jim heap Mexican. Where Red Wolf? Chief want him."

"Colonel Smith!" instantly called out his companion, "I played Greaser to git through their lines. How'd you do it?"

"That young Lipan wolf did it," he said. "He led us 'round to the west'ard, and we hadn't anything to do but to follow him. They thought our party was one of their own patrols. We didn't lose a man. Colonel Bonham got in all alone."

No more explanations could be given then

and there, for Carson had made his daring experiment that he might bring encouraging despatches from the President and that he might not break his word about returning.

Travis opened the letter handed him and he read it where he stood.

"It's all right, men,' he said. "The whole state is rising. If we can hold the fort a little longer the boys 'll come!"

Hearty cheers responded, and Carson was at once taken possession of by his fellow-rangers that they might pump him of all the news he had gathered while away.

"Ugh! Heap boy!" said Castro.

Before him stood Red Wolf, and during two or three minutes they talked rapidly in their own tongue. As soon as the chief ceased speaking, Travis approached him and held out a hand.

"Glad Travis no dead," said Castro, heartily. "Where Big Knife? Where Crockett?"

"Here we are!" responded the latter from a little behind him. "But what on all the 'arth fetched you into the fort jest now? Did the Greasers say you might come a-visitin'?"

The Lipan warrior turned on his heel and

stalked away to the battered patch of the wall, followed by his white friends. He stepped up upon the heap of ruins and studied it for a moment.

"Castro see Mexican," he said. "See Bravo. Heap friend. Lipans no fight 'em. Tell 'em all Lipans lie down in lodge. Tell Bravo walk through wall. Come back. Tell Mexican. Bravo say, Castro go see fort. Now! Ugh! Tell Travis, tell Big Knife, one sleep. Mexican come take Texan hair."

"Jest so," replied Crockett. "They're goin' to try that hole to-morrow morning? We'll pile it high with Greasers."

"All right, chief," added Travis, "tell them all they want to know. It's a fair trade for letting us know they're coming. You can't tell anything to hurt us."

"Ugh!" said Castro. "Chief take Red Wolf. Go hide in Santa Anna camp. See fight. Boy go tell Houston how Travis."

"Good!" replied Travis. "Just the thing. Let him set out as soon as the fight is over. I'd like to have old Sam know just how it turns out. So far, we've beaten 'em every time."

"Castro heap friend," said the chief, and

took from under his blanket a deerskin-covered parcel closely tied. " Big Knife want powder. Take present. Shoot heap."

About two pounds of the best rifle powder, therefore, was his last contribution to the defence of the fort.

" Now if that isn't just what we wanted !" shouted Crockett. " I say, Bowie, divide fair. I've only five charges myself. Pistols empty."

Some of the others were as badly off, and shortly afterwards it might have been noted that Bowie's belt fairly bristled with the short-barrelled but deadly weapons known as " Derringers," from the name of their manufacturer.

"There is going to be a use for them," he quietly remarked to Travis. " If I'm not mistaken, every bullet 'll find a mark to-morrow."

" Look out," returned Travis. " Don't you go and get yourself only wounded."

" No !" almost shouted Bowie. " But what if I am ? Could I quit if there was a breath of life left in me ? Travis, they don't intend to take any prisoners."

"There won't be any to take," he replied, but his friend drew him aside, farther out of any risk of being heard by others.

"One thing more," said Bowie. "I want to get together all the men that went down into Mexico with me. Crockett, too. The chief and his son are going. They don't count just now. They'll never tell anyhow, but somebody ought to live and keep that treasure-secret. It must be found for Texas some day."

"We might draw cuts for a man to get away with it," suggested Travis, "but he'd have no chance. I don't see what we can do. You and I are sure to go down."

Castro and Red Wolf were standing by their ponies in the plaza. They were not members of the garrison. They were not white citizens of Texas. There was no reason why they should remain to meet the last onset of Santa Anna's army. Each of them had done all that he could for his personal friendships.

"Ugh!" said Castro. "No want more shake hand. Come. Go talk Bravo. Tell Mexican heap. Great chief lose friend. Ugh!"

The gate had been opened for them and they mounted at once, but as they were passing through the portal Red Wolf turned and took a swift, earnest survey of the interior of the fort. It was all quiet, all peaceful. The cannon watched silently at their embrasures. The rangers walked hither and thither unconcernedly. The church front wore a calm and placid look. The sun was shining brightly. The one dark spot full of evil omen was the heap of rubbish in the breach of the wall.

"Ugh!" said Red Wolf, mournfully. "Big Knife fight a heap. Great chief!"

More than one demand for surrender had been sent in and had been rejected. During several days, however, any other communication with the fort had been strictly forbidden. The Mexican general, nevertheless, had not been unwilling to permit the visit of Castro, and when the chief returned now, he speedily found himself in front of Santa Anna's marquee.

"Heap boy in fort," he replied to a question from General Sesma. "Great chief go get him. Red Wolf no Texan. Good!"

There was no apparent importance in the presence or absence of one unarmed young Indian, and Santa Anna hardly looked at him while he questioned his father closely concerning the aspect of affairs in the fort. There was no use to the garrison to be gained by Castro's concealment of anything that a telescope in the camp could discover, but the Mexican commander exhibited a deep interest iu the exact character and dimensions of the hole his artillery had made in the wall.

" *Caramba !*" exclaimed Castrillon. " I'll pitch a few more shot into it in the morning. How many of the rebels have we killed ?"

" Texan feel good !" replied Castro. " Big gun no hurt him."

Many and loud were the execrations uttered when he explained himself further and positively affirmed that all their cannonading and musketry had not disabled a solitary Texan.

" We shall do better to-morrow," said Santa Anna, with a cynical grin. " How are their provisions ?"

" Little eat," said Castro. " Texan lie in fort. No make fire. No kettle."

" Short of rations, eh ?" said General Cos. " That's a point, general. We might starve 'em out. We have lost a great many men——"

" We had better lose twice as many," sharply interrupted his commander, " than to waste any more time here. Houston is getting his volunteers in hand. We must have the Alamo to-morrow if it costs us a thousand men !"

"What Santa Anna say now to great chief?" asked Castro. "What tell Lipan?"

His inquiry was made somewhat haughtily, but the response came at once with extreme graciousness and courtesy. The Lipans were to consider themselves the fast friends of the Mexican republic, their chief was to call himself the brother of its President, and Castro and Red Wolf were led away to a camp-fire where plentiful rations awaited them. It was not a time when the invaders of Texas were willing to make additional enemies.

It was not altogether a cheerful time for them. Really, the greatest element of uncertainty of success in the proposed assault of the fort was the dispirited, defeated feeling that prevailed among the Mexican troops. It was to obviate that defect in their fighting qualities that Colonel Campos, of the infantry, received orders that night to issue liberal rations of *aguardiente,* or Mexican whiskey, as soon as the several battalions should march into their respective positions.

"Colonel," said Santa Anna, "their feathers are down a little. Make them so drunk they won't know whether they are killed or not.

Who cares? We have plenty to take their places if we win a victory."

More *peones* and *rancheros* could be expended to any extent provided he could retain his autocratic grip upon the reins of power.

There were one hundred and eighty-seven persons within the walls of the fort that night. Six of these were non-combatants, including two American women, a Mexican woman, a negro slave, and two young children.

The keepers of the secret of the cavern of Huitzilopochtli held their conference. After it was concluded they selected, with careful deliberation, a number of trustworthy men, to whom, under oath, they communicated the precious information. If any or all of them should survive, a full report was to be in like manner made to President Houston and other Texan patriots who were named.

"That's all we can do," remarked Bowie, after his precautions had been taken. "I don't want that expedition to die with me. If any of these fellows are killed early in the fight, we must put in others in their places."

"All right," replied Crockett. "The Montezumas have stuck to that stuff long enough.

But, 'cordin' to Castro, we've been and gone and put a death-warrant on every one of those men. I was thinking 'bout that."

"You'd think!" exclaimed Bowie, "if you'd seen what I did. Do you know, there was the queerest kind of roar coming up out of that chasm. I don't wonder the blood-thirsty heathen were superstitious about it."

"I'd like to hear it some day," said Crockett. "But thar's a kind of ringing in my ears, anyhow. Perhaps it's from hearing so much cannon music."

In the cavern of Huitzilopochtli that night, the treasure-chamber of the Montezumas, the voice from the lower deep was calling more loudly than usual.

"The gods are disturbed," grumbled the old men before the altar. "We have nothing to give them. They grow angry. What shall we do for the hunger of the gods?"

Louder, at intervals, then seeming to die away and begin again, arose the mysterious reverberation, while the old devotees paused from their chanting to turn and glare into each other's ferocious faces.

It was only a mute inquiry. If no other

supply should be provided, to which of them would belong the next voluntary plunge into the gulf?

They were fewer than they once had been. There might be none to take their places. It would not do for the altar of Huitzilopochtli to be left without servitors and the treasure without guardians. Some of them must remain until the return of the gods, for these were surely to come again to claim their own.

Why, however, should they at this time feel so strong a hunger and send up so vehement an outcry? Had they heard that sacrifices were about to come? If so, where were the expected victims, and whose hand should bring them?

It was a question to which no answer could be given, but the sacrificial fire was heaped with fuel until its radiance flickered like a smile of satisfaction upon the vast, dark face on the wall, and the priests chanted on with a croaking sound like that of many ravens.

No morning ever came into that cavern, but it dawned brightly upon the outside world,— the morning of the 6th of March, 1836.

The camp of the Mexican army was astir at

an early hour and the artillery began its practice-work upon the shattered wall. Every gun was aimed with care, for even Santa Anna was using up the last of his cannon-shot.

There was apparently nothing doing in the fort. It had a lazy look, and the rangers hardly spoke to one another as they went about their routine duties. They all cleaned their rifles carefully, counted their bullets, measured their charges of powder, and now and then they would stroll to loop-holes for looks at the Mexican camp.

"They are forming for the attack," was the word that passed from man to man, while the iron missiles, fairly well directed, fell fast upon the frail barrier which had been made at the breach.

"There 'll a good many men drap in that thar gap," remarked Crockett. "But they won't all try to come in by that way."

The Mexican commander had indeed learned something by experience. His storming columns were four in number, and only one of them advanced toward the broken wall. Another was evidently to approach by the front, where the ruins of the gate had been strongly

propped up during the night.   The third and
fourth formed in front of the convent yard
wall and the church, and their ladders would
be quite long enough to carry them over the
former.

"We've got to divide," said Travis.   "You
hold the convent and church side, Bowie.
They could pick their way in, or blast a hole,
if you'd let 'em.   We'll take care of the rest."

Only a few men could be spared to any of
the several posts of danger.

The Mexican batteries ceased.   The half-
drunken infantry came on at a run.   The last
cartridges were rapidly and effectively fired
from the Texan cannon.   Down went their
enemies by scores, and it looked as if the pre-
vions results were to be repeated, but Sergeant
Daly now stepped back from the gun he had
been working and held up a hand.

"All gone!" exclaimed Travis.   "Come on,
men, this four-pounder is loaded yet.   Let's
bring it to bear upon the breach and give it to
them as they come through."

The guns on the church, three in number,
had also been busy, but they now ceased their
thunder.   Down went the gate before the blows

20

óf the Mexican pioneers. Fast fell the fore-most assailants in the fatal breach, but just as Travis had swung around his cannon a mus-keteer from the gate was within twenty feet of him.   He did not miss.   The calm, courageous smile upon the face of the heroic commander died away, for the flying lead passed through his brain.

Numbers counted now, for the enemy were within the walls, and the remaining struggle was hand-to-hand.

Brave enough were the Mexicans, but they were learning terrible lessons of the superior personal prowess of their victims.   Not a man asked for quarter.   To be only wounded and to fall was to be bayoneted upon the ground.   Five who were disabled did indeed take refuge in the cook-room, barring its door and fighting still.

Half-way between the convent and the church a thick group of swordsmen and lan-cers closed around the old bear hunter, but he did not die alone.   Near him lay half a dozen of his foemen, and just beyond them fell his old friends Smith and Bonham, hastening to die at his side.

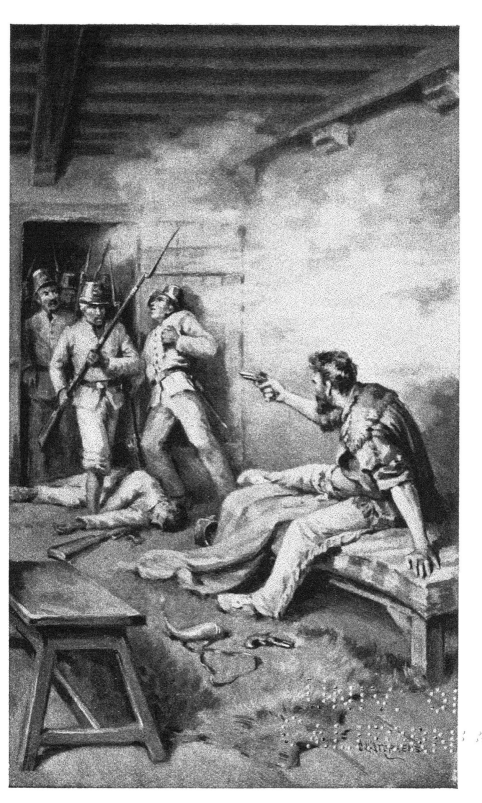

A dark, stern, terrible shape half rose from a couch.

The last squad of riflemen stood in front of the main inside entrance of the fort building, plying their rifles steadily, but the surge of steel points poured towards them.

"Boys!" exclaimed Bowie at their head, "I'm hurt in the leg. I can't stand. I must do the rest of it lying down."

His empty rifle fell from his hand as he climbed a stairway near him. Bleeding and faint, he staggered on to the end of a passage, and he threw himself upon the couch in the end room, exclaiming,—

"I saw them fall! Not a man is left to tell the secret of the cavern!"

It was but a moment, and then the passage-way swarmed with furious Mexicans. From room to room they went, plying their bayonets alike upon the living and the dead. As they entered the corner room, however, a dark, stern, terrible shape half rose from a couch with a Derringer in its right hand. Swift reports followed each other as rapidly as the tickings of a clock till Bowie's belt was empty. The floor was strewn with corpses, and then, as yet more of his enemies poured in, he gained his feet with a last effort, knife in hand.

It was but for a moment. It was the fierce agony of a dying hero. The bayonets did their work, and as the stalwart form of the dead borderer sank heavily upon the floor, a low voice in the door-way exclaimed,—

"Big Knife! Heap brave! Great chief! Red Wolf go."

The Alamo had fallen!

The five men in the cook-room surrendered to Castrillon when their last cartridge was gone on promise of protection, but they were sabred at once on being taken before Santa Anna, who now stood among his staff in the middle of the plaza.

"*Caramba!* Kill them!" was all the reply he made to the protests of Castrillon.

The six non-combatants were spared to tell the story of the defence and the massacre, but the victory had been a costly one. The army of Santa Anna had been so shattered that, when he met Sam Houston and his volunteers, not many days later, at San Jacinto, his eighteen hundred men were utterly defeated by about a third of their number of Texans, and he lost not only his army of invasion but his control of Mexican affairs, and Texas itself.

Dark indeed, that day, was the cavern of Huitzilopochtli, and all through the early hours the moaning sound came up from the chasm. Then it grew louder, stronger, and the worshippers fled from its brink to the altar. They had no victims to offer. Their chant was almost drowned by the ominous roar, and the hungry anger of the gods seemed to increase momentarily. Then it began to die away,— away,—until at last a kind of shout came up, and there was a silence. Excepting Red Wolf and his father, there were now no living persons, outside of the votaries of the old faith, who had any clue to the hidden treasure and the underground temple of the lost gods of Mexico. The daring Texan who had learned the secret had fallen fighting to the end, the last man of the garrison of the Alamo.

THE END.

ELECTROTYPED AND PRINTED BY J. B. LIPPINCOTT COMPANY, PHILADELPHIA, U.S.A.

The Mystery of the Island.

By HENRY KINGSLEY.

A Tale of Bush and Pampas, Wreck, and Treasure Trove. By the author of "Geoffrey Hamlyn," "Ravenshoe," etc., etc. A new edition, with illustrations by Warne Browne. 12mo. Cloth, $1.25.

The Wizard King.

By DAVID KER.

Crown 8vo. Cloth, $1.50.

"It is based upon careful study of history, is written graphically and even brilliantly, is absorbing from cover to cover, and has an excellent moral tone It deserves to be a lasting favorite with the young people "—*Boston Congregationalist.*

Hugh Melville's Quest.

By F. M. HOLMES.

Illustrated. 12mo. Cloth, $1.25.

"Well written volumes that describe ancient history in an interesting manner are to be always welcomed. This volume will serve a good purpose by recalling days that were of prime importance in the making of the English nation "—*New York School Journal.*

J. B. LIPPINCOTT COMPANY, PHILADELPHIA.

By CAPTAIN CHARLES KING, U. S. A.

Trooper Ross and Signal Butte.

Illustrated by Charles S. Stephens.

Crown 8vo. Cloth, $1.50

When Captain King sets his hand to a boy's story he is sure to be an ideal creator of heroes. Redskins and blue-jackets, and lovely girls and daring youngsters are in his dramatic company; camp-fires, blazing villages, rifle-reports, and narrow escapes. He is never coarse nor sensational, but with his sweeping style carries you on from start to finish like a stiff and wholesome breeze.

"They are just the stories to captivate the young reader."—*Philadelphia Evening Bulletin.*

"Captain Charles King has never written more captivating stories of frontier life than the two that are embraced in this neat volume just issued."—*San Francisco Bulletin*

"Captain King has done many good things, but perhaps none better than these animated tales, which are full of Indians, good and bad, scouts, cowboys, and everything needful to keep a restless boy quiet on an evening"—*Philadelphia Evening Telegraph.*

"The list of Captain King's books for boys is in itself calculated to excite youthful imaginations and hold their attention unrelaxed to the close. These two latest stories contain all the striking features of its predecessors, the excitement, the fire, the geniality, the rapidity that have long delighted his large community of boy readers."—*Boston Courier.*

J. B. LIPPINCOTT COMPANY, PHILADELPHIA.

The Boys' Own Book of In-Door Games and Recreations.

A POPULAR ENCYCLOPÆDIA FOR BOYS.

Edited by G. A. Hutchinson.

With over 700 illustrations.   528 pages. $1 75.

It is especially a boy's book, calculated to afford both pleasure and profit, treating of those topics in which boys take particular interest.   There are chapters on gymnastic exercises, games, and sports of all kinds; the boy's workshop; how to build boats, etc.; musical instruments; toys; conjurers and conjuring; ventriloquism; and pleasant and profitable occupation for spare hours.

" It gives the boys such instruction as they like, and will keep many an active boy employed in his workshop and away from a companionship that is hurtful   It is both a useful and a beautiful book "—*Chicago Inter-Ocean*

Boys' Own Book of Out-Door Sports.

UNIFORM WITH BOYS' OWN BOOK OF IN-DOOR SPORTS.

Illustrated   1 vol.   4to   *Cloth, gilt, $1 75*

Containing articles on swimming, boating, cycling, hare and hounds, skating, lawn-tennis, foot-ball, etc.   In short, an encyclopædia of just those things which boys want to know about.

" This is a capital book," says the *New York Independent*.   " The illustrations, diagrams, and drawings are very numerous and excellent, and the subject is treated in every aspect and variety by competent writers, who describe well and have the art of lending a charm to their dullest details."

J. B. LIPPINCOTT COMPANY, PHILADELPHIA.

The Girls' Own In-Door Book.

CONTAINING PRACTICAL HELP TO GIRLS ON ALL MATTERS
RELATING TO THEIR MATERIAL COMFORT AND WELL-BEING

Edited by Charles Peters.

With over 150 illustrations. 548 pages Square 12mo. Cloth extra, $1.75.

"It gives illustrated directions for acquiring a wide variety of practical and ornamental arts, deals with health and etiquette, and all is set forth with refinement, taste, and good sense."—*New York Tribune.*

"No more welcome present for a girl just getting into her teens could be found than this fine, well-filled volume—a perfect storehouse of information and amusement. It tells how to do everything a girl would like to do, and to do it well, from tatting to playing the violin or organ."—*St. Louis Republic.*

The Girls' Own Out-Door Book.

Edited by Charles Peters,

EDITOR OF ' THE GIRLS' OWN IN-DOOR BOOK."

180 illustrations. 510 pages Square 12mo. Cloth extra, $1.75.

CONTENTS.—Girlhood; Out-Door Recreations; The Sea-Side; Our Summer Holidays; Holiday Needle-Work; Social Amusements; Etiquette; Travelling; Shopping and Marketing; The Gardener; Fowl Rearing; The Botanist; The Ornithologist; Knick-Knacks made from Natural Objects; Photography; Astronomy; Out-Door Music; Christian Work.

"All that the work contains is set forth with refinement, taste, and good sense "—*New York Tribune.*

"With such a table of contents, no right-minded and intelligent girl can fail to reap pleasure and profit from a careful study of this volume."—*San Francisco Bulletin.*

"A handsome volume that will carry pleasure and profit where it goes."—*Philadelphia Ledger.*

"Let this book be found in every household where there are girls."—*Rochester* (*N. Y.*) *Rural Home.*

J. B. LIPPINCOTT COMPANY, PHILADELPHIA.

By GEORGE MORGAN.

John Littlejohn, of J.

BEING IN PARTICULAR AN
ACCOUNT OF HIS REMARKABLE ENTANGLEMENT WITH THE KING'S
INTRIGUES AGAINST GENERAL WASHINGTON.

12mo.   Cloth extra, deckle edges, $1.25.

"George Morgan's style is strong and free, intensely literal and vividly poetic by turns, and he has prepared himself thoroughly by knowing the scenes and studying the historic incidents with the pains necessary for a good historic novel. 'John Littlejohn, of J.,' is a tale of Revolutionary times. It opens at Valley Forge, introducing amid lesser-known officers, Americans and their French and German allies, Washington, of course, and Hamilton and Conway, the cabalist, the noble young Lafayette, Baron Steuben, and others of distinction. Out-and-out adventure, intrigues, with their plot and counterplot, the romance of maiden's love, smoothing the horrors and compensating for the dangers and discomforts of grim war, are here well mingled. The story ends at the battle of Monmouth, in which the treachery of Lee, and Washington's one recorded oath when he denounced and insulted Lee by the word and sign 'Poltroon,' as understood between soldier and soldier, and by his superb presence turned defeat into victory, are told with spirit."
—*Boston Evening Transcript.*

"'John Littlejohn, of J.,' is a story full of originality, of vitality, action, and charming bits of descriptive writing; an earnest, able, and highly interesting picture of the American Revolution, a romance which must always find an honored place among the comparatively few novels having a background of American history . . . The style is a wonder of crispness and of a kind of Shakespearian happiness The spirit is remarkable, as is also the fidelity to the times, to place, and to character."—*Philadelphia Inquirer.*

J. B. LIPPINCOTT COMPANY, PHILADELPHIA.

A Comic History of
the United States

By BILL NYE.

With one hundred and fifty illustrations by
F. OPPER.

12mo. Cloth extra, $2.00.

CLUB LIFE IN EARLY NEW YORK

" The author's satire is keen, his humor unceasing, but he never has forgotten the requirements of good taste. The book will induce many a smile and not a few uproarious laughs."—*Philadelphia Evening Bulletin.*

" Those who admire the funniments of Bill Nye will enjoy many a hearty laugh at his quaint and curious way of presenting historical facts."—*Boston Saturday Evening Gazette.*

"One cannot forbear a smile over these truly comic sketches."—*Public Ledger*, Philadelphia.

" Everybody with any sense of humor in their souls will be entertained—and instructed, too—by its perusal "—*Boston Home Journal.*

" The greatest enjoyment will be derived from it "—*Chicago Journal.*

" The book is bound to be a great success."—*New York School Journal.*

" The best thing Bill Nye has ever done. There is real worth in it."—*Philadelphia To-Day.*

J. B. LIPPINCOTT COMPANY, PHILADELPHIA.

M̄18908

Lightning Source UK Ltd.
Milton Keynes UK
UKHW020752110219
337098UK00014B/1402/P